M000167271

If Only

If Only

OLUSEYI
J. AKINLADE

 PYXIDIA HOUSE PUBLISHERS

If Only

Copyright©2022 by Oluseyi J. Akinlade

Scripture quotations are from the Holy Bible: King James Version (KJV), New King James Version (NJKV), The Message (MSG), New International Version (NIV), New Living Translation (NLT).

Request for information on this title should be addressed to

Oluseyi J. Akinlade
Email: oluakins1@gmail.com

Library of Congress Cataloging-in-Publication Data

Oluseyi J. Akinlade
If Only
ISBN-13: 978-1-946530-38-7 (Paperback)
ISBN-10: 1-946530-38-7 (Paperback)
1. Religious - Fiction 1. Title
Library of Congress Control Number: 2022951666

Edited by Winnie Aduayi

Published in Dallas Texas by Pyxidia House Publishers. A registered trademark of Pyxidia Concept llc.
www.pyxidiahouse.com   info@pyxidiahouse.com

Printed in the United States of America

To Almighty God
who alone is worthy of my praise.

To the gifts in my life:
my beautiful wife, Omowunmi Akinlade,
and my three God-fearing children –
Daniel, Esther, and Enoch.

Acknowledgement

I give all the Glory to the Most High God for the writing and publishing of this book.

My special appreciation goes to two of my fathers in the Lord, Rev. Olusegun Martins and Dr. Wole Adeyi for their fatherly advice, encouragement, and support in the writing of this book.

Also, to Evangelist Lolo, for all your support and encouragement.

Lastly, I want to appreciate my Editor, Winnie, and everyone at Pyxidia House for all your hard work in making this dream come true.

Contents

Then Jesus said, "Come to me, all of you who
are weary and carry heavy burdens,
and I will give you rest"
– Matthew 11:28 (NLT)

Prologue

Philip stood by the window in his office shaded by a huge, old tree, listening to the birds and watching the puffy white clouds travel across the blue sky on a cool September morning. Every morning before heading out for the day's job and in his free time, he loved to stand here, listening to the bees' buzz, smelling the fragrant flowers, and helping himself to a cup of coffee. It is the beginning of fall, the leaves have started changing colors, and the sky looks beautiful with blue, gold, and silk-white lines around it. With the ray of sunlight gently peeking through the cloudy blue sky, it felt like he could almost smell the scent of the ray's beauty, the beauty of the handwork of God. As he stood there gazing from his office window, enveloped in the beauty of God's creation, he suddenly felt the urge to go for a walk.

He walked over to his desk and closed his laptop lid after scanning through the jobs for the day; he had quite a few plumbing jobs downtown LA but the first one wasn't until 12noon, so he had some time. He grabbed his wallet and headed out the door, asking his secretary, Maggie, to page him for any urgent calls from the clients. He was wearing a pair of blue jeans, a red polo T-shirt with a black jacket, and black work boots. This outfit was far from what he would ordinarily wear for the long walk he had in mind.

As Philip walked along the railroad path, he noticed what looked like a shiny object in the middle of one of the rails far away from where he was. And just like Moses in the Bible when he saw the burning bush, he was curious to see what it was. On getting to the spot, he realized the shining object was a young lady wearing a light, bright white sweater passed out on the rail tracks. A dizzying number of questions flooded his mind at once. What?! Is this a dream? What is she doing out here alone? What happened to her? Why is she in the middle of the rail – is she trying to get herself killed? He wasn't sure if to touch her or not;

several thoughts raced through his head. Philip stood, confused about what to do; he thought to call someone; she may be dying or dead. Then, she moved slightly, and then with much effort, she tried to crawl forward on her stomach but couldn't. She appeared too weak, and her lips were parched, like someone extremely dehydrated.

"Oh, thank you, Lord; she's alive," Philip mumbled; his hand ferreted around in his pockets for his phone. He dialed 911.

And as he heard the sirens from afar, the sight of her laying there all alone, close to death, took him down memory lane to the story of a young lady called Roseline...

Chapter One

It was a perfect July day as the sun came up over the city, and Roseline watched it from her patio. She sat looking at blue, pink, and orange streaks across the sky as she stretched out, happily rocking her little frame on her mother's sun-faded rocking chair, gifted her by Roseline's dad when they got married. The pretty jet black-haired, exuberant Roseline sat in the golden light of the sunrise as the early summer sun shot copper lights through her long, stretched hair, which hung nearly below her shoulders. She was wearing an old flannel nightgown with barely discernible hearts on it, and her feet were bare. The house she lived in sat on a plateau in Corpus Christi, Texas, overlooking the ocean and narrow beach below. This was exactly where Roseline wanted to be with her family. She had lived here for three years. This seemingly tiny forgotten beach community suited her perfectly.

Calling her home a house was generous. It was barely more than a cottage, but the place made her happy nonetheless, as it was filled with happy memories that she and her mother had created. It was incomprehensible to her mother, though, why Roseline would want to live there forever as she often said or how she would even love it as much as she did. But Roseline was a happy child who found contentment in even the smallest things, and she dreamily looked forward to creating more beautiful memories in that home with her father, who was yet to meet her, when he returned home.

Roseline was born a few months after her father, Ronald, was deployed for military service. Ronald enlisted in the US Army during their senior year in high school, and a few months after he got married to his high school sweetheart, Sophie, he was deployed to Kuwait during the Persian Gulf war, nicknamed *Operation Desert Storm*, in response to the invasion of Kuwait in 1990. Her parents, Ronald and Sophie, had met while in high school, though they attended different schools. They had first met during one of their summer vacations when they visited their grandparents who happened to live in the same town. However, at that time, none of them had a chance to say a word to each other under the constant watchful eyes of Sophie's grandparents, but as fate would have it, they met again at one of their interschool sports events. Sophie happened to be one of the field and track stars for her school, while Ronald was one of the soccer players for his school team. It was at this event that the fire of their love was ignited, and from that moment on, their love continued to grow like a wildfire.

Sophie was a young woman with the sweetness of girlhood yet stepping with confidence into the shoes of womanhood in her queenly figure. She has copper-brown skin, like a windfall autumn leaf, perfectly complementing her smoldering, doe-brown eyes and jet-black hair that caresses her pinched-in cheekbones. Sophie was only fifteen and more than a little dazzled by Ronald's tall, dark, midwestern good looks and charm. He was clean-shaven, his face ever so smooth, and he had nappy jet-black hair that he kept very low-cut, and bright brown eyes. Ronald was a great young man and did everything he was supposed to do – he did well in school, was kind and loving, and still had enough mischief in him to reassure his peers he was normal; he had a good sense of humor and a fine mind. Like Sophie, Ronald was a country boy and only a year older than she was. Sophie's mother had kept a watchful eye on them, afraid that Sophie would fall too madly in love and do something foolish. But Ronald had been respectful of her and as much in love as Sophie. Ronald was the epitome of a nice guy, at least so he was before his deployment.

Sophie was fresh out of school when she married Ronald and did not have a job after her wedding before Ronald left. She became very lonely without Ronald; she missed him every day, and to deal with her loneliness, she started volunteer work at the kindergarten in her neighborhood. Three months after he left, she discovered she was pregnant; it was unexpected as they had planned to wait, so she decided to keep the good news as a surprise gift for Ronald when he returned home. In all of their conversations, she worked hard not to spill the good news of his baby growing within her, eagerly awaiting his return in a few short months, but then, three months soon became six and six became indefinite months, and the phone calls got even less frequent right after she had their baby girl, Roseline.

The birth of their baby girl kept her occupied and helped fill the void Ronald's extended absence had created while still loving him the same as ever, and when Roseline turned two, Sophie began teaching the Art program at the Kindergarten Roseline attended. Ronald was in Kuwait for 36 months, 16 months of which he spent in hospital recovering from war injuries that cost him his left leg, which he chose to keep from Sophie until he returned; he wanted her to see him as he is now, not to be told over the phone. They both had something to share, but when he returned things were never the same for Roseline's parents, Ronald and Sophie.

There were nights Ronald dreamed in such vivid detail that he would wake up screaming and throwing things at no one in particular and then curl up like a foetus and weep while Sophie would try to gather him in her arms, but he would yell at her to leave him alone. At other times when he woke, he was confused, forgetting where he was for a fraction of a second. For the minutes that followed, he felt the grief all over, the loss of things he never even considered missing. He'd never been one to dwell on things and laze in dreams – fantasy was never his thing. He'd been all action, all hero, never slowing for even a day, but all he does now is dwell in lazy thoughts, uncontrollable fits of rage, and deep sadness. Once the sadness became less acute, he'd reach for his crotches and slowly limp his way to the kitchen, where he remembered cooking, laughing, and eating with Sophie but now no longer enjoyed. Everything was still the same in the kitchen as when he left for Kuwait; the walls were golden stone, the floor tiles the color of summer baked earth, the fixtures off-white porcelain. Not much had changed in the kitchen, but everything had changed in their lives. As a military officer, he knew well the value of self-discipline, self-control and making choices compatible with empathy and logic. That makes it so emotionally challenging, making life or death calls whilst the heart had to feel it all; this wasn't easy to deal with, so Ronald thrust all his pain and anger against Sophie's love and the love their daughter, Roseline, offers in her innocence.

One Saturday afternoon, while Roseline and her

mom were sitting in the living room watching TV, her dad walked in.

"Welcome dad," said Roseline.

"Hey! How many times have I told you not to call me dad? I am not your dad!" Ronald yelled angrily.

Roseline, shocked and upset at her dad's mean response, rushed to her room crying.

Now hearing that, her mom jumped up from the couch, "Honey! What is wrong with you, how can you say that to an innocent child?" She questioned, hurt and looking straight into his eyes.

"Say what?!" He retorted with a mocking laughter, taking a step back, "Do your math, and tell me if she's mine." He exploded defiantly and looked away as he saw the hurt in her eyes.

"Has the military service injected something into your head that is affecting your brain? Or are you just a wicked soul?" Roseline's mother said calmly, pain threading every word and tears rolling down her cheeks.

Hearing these words, he came at her angrily, grabbed her by the neck and threw her down on the couch, "You're a filthy liar! I'm a trained military man, and I can kill with my bare hands, next time you try this nonsense with me, I will kill you!" He said to her coldly, got up and limped away with his crotches, leaving Roseline confused and hurt.

Though Roseline had seen her parents argue on several occasions, but this was the first time she ever witnessed a physical altercation between them. She had no idea what was going on with her dad emotionally and or psychologically, neither did her mother, Sophie. But from Sophie's little understanding of Post-Traumatic Stress Disorder (PTSD), she suspected he was fighting an invisible enemy within; an enemy that is much bigger and stronger than himself. She was so sad to see her once happy and loving Ronald, and their home turning upside down in the twinkle of an eye.

"Whatever happens, I am your co-warrior; I am here to fight this battle with you, Ron. Please, let me in, don't shut me out." She said in the softest voice she could muster, tears streaming down her cheeks.

But her words fell on deaf ears as he limped out of the house and slammed the door on them. She lowered herself to the wooden floor, pulling her little girl, Roseline, into her arms, and rocking her gently, as tears continue to roll down her cheeks, and she got lost in her thoughts: Aren't battles always fought to ensure we all have what we need to live in peace and thrive? This battle in Kuwait surely has fetched the opposite.

Chapter Two

The doorbell rang at six o'clock and broke Sophie's reverie; she was in their little kitchen reminiscing over the good times she'd shared with Ronald, and in her hand was the last letter from him while in Kuwait shortly before his return home. It must be Robin Weatherford, she thought. Robin was a young, overly ambitious private salesman she had recently contacted about selling some of her things to raise some money; she was running out of money since she'd never had a steady source of income except what she used to get from Ronald. She was hoping that if she sold all her jewelry, including the gold set that Ronald had given her as a wedding gift, she might be able to cater for her and Roseline's needs, pending when she could be emotionally stable to work an actual job. Outside of the jewelry sales, she had no idea how she would support herself and Roseline. For the moment, all she could do was hope that the tides would turn, and Ronald would return to his senses, back to them, his family. But for now, she would just get through each day, keep living and do her best not to drown in sorrow.

Roseline was in her room doing her homework or pretending to be doing that just to stay out of her mother's way, who seemed to be provoked at every little thing these days. She was in middle school now, 12 years old, and had to take care of herself most of the time. School seemed to be her only escape, though it wasn't much of an escape as it got harder. Her elementary school year was like a walk in the park; going through middle school, on the other hand, was not as easy as she had thought. Sophie had planned to make dinner late for them, which gave her time to brood as she sat in the kitchen and got startled when she heard the doorbell.

She was only expecting Robin Weatherford with his estimate when she went to the door, but she saw their former neighbor, Tim Brooks, through the peephole. He was alone and wearing light blue jeans and a black T-shirt, with his hair neatly trimmed. She opened the door with a look of surprise; he seemed hesitant until she asked him to come in. Tim, always too well-mannered, she thought. He saw a look of strain in her eyes, her hair unkempt, and she seemed weary. He wondered what was bothering her as she looked like she had the weight of the world on her shoulders. But as he walked in, she smiled and tried to be pleasant.

"Hello Tim, been a while. How are you?" She asked with a tired smile.

"I'm doing good, thank you for asking," Tim responded. After an uncomfortable silence, Tim continued, "I'm sorry to bother you; I wanted to stop by to speak to you."

He glanced around the untidy sitting room; it was hard not to be unimpressed by the state of the house, his eyes finally resting on her unkempt appearance. He'd never known her to be careless and untidy; she appeared deeply troubled. Her grief was stamped all over her.

"So, you wanted to see me about something?" She asked as she gestured for him to sit on one of the couches.

"Ronald called me today... I'm not sure why he chose to call me, though... but he did," he stuttered, with some sadness clouding his eyes.

Sophie panicked and no longer pretended to be okay, "Is Ron all right? Talk to me. What's going on?"

"I don't know how best to say this. I was surprised to get a call from Ronald earlier this morning; I hadn't heard from him in a few months," Tim hesitated, watching her every move and expression; there was something both strong and fragile about her, and it was odd to see her so sad. "He called me from the hospital to meet with him.... but I couldn't get to him until after my shift at work, and when...."

"And when what? What happened to Ron?" Sophie screamed wide-eyed, grabbing his T-shirt, and at the sound of her voice, Roseline rushed out of her room into the living room.

"What is it, mom... Mr. Brooks?" Roseline asked, looking from one to the other.

"Talk to me, Tim; what has happened to Ron?"

He looked up at Roseline and back at Sophie questioningly.

"It's okay; you can speak in her presence; please talk to me... and when what?" She said, her heart pounding so fast and hard with fear written all over her face.

"When I finally got to the hospital, I barely said hello to him, and he began to code, then the doctors rushed in and sent me out of the room. He was gone a few minutes later; I didn't get to hear what he wanted to say. I was too late. I'm so sorry, Sophie," he said, bursting into tears, as he gathered her up in his arms, and Roseline slid down to the floor shocked and teary.

After a while, Sophie found her composure; freeing herself from his embrace, she went over to Roseline, sat beside her, and gathered her in a tight embrace, rocking her gently as she used to before Ronald disrupted their once-happy lives with his pain, anger, and distrust.

"What happened to him?" She asked quietly, looking up at Tim.

"A hit-and-run driver hit him; it was on a lonely road; no one saw anything. And the doctors also found much alcohol in his system. He'd been in surgery, and it was successful, but then this. I thought you should hear from me before the police come over." He said helplessly.

Sophie releasing Roseline, doubled over in gut wrenching cry. She wept with deep sorrow for the man she'd lost long before this day; she wept for everything they all lost for no justifiable reason and all they could have had so freely. Indeed, the devil comes to steal, to kill, and to destroy; he took it all from her and their innocent child, Roseline, who was conceived in pure love, yet denied that same love.

Ronald was rarely home the past few months leading up to his death, and when he did come home, he treated Sophie like a horrible disease; he couldn't stand to look at her or say a kind word to her, and he would leave at the first crack of dawn. His absence from home got longer with each outing; he had not been home the past three weeks, and Sophie had looked everywhere for him to no avail. Resentful, lonely, and afraid, she had become a shadow of herself and taken to the bottle.

It's been six months since Ronald's burial; Sophie does nothing now but drink, throw fits of rage, and mope around the house. Standing in the middle of the living room at 6.30am Monday, Sophie felt like she was going to pass out with a blinding headache, having cried all night and drowned herself in whiskey, which seemed to be her favorite thing since Ronald's death snatched away all hope of reconciliation with him. She slid backwards and steadied herself against the wall.

"I have to go; I can't take it anymore," she whispered to herself, her eyes hollow and blank.

The voices came back, *"Yes, go, Sophie. Buy more drinks and get it over with. Ronald will never love you or touch ever you again; he is gone, and no one loves you; no one will miss you. Not even Roseline: she wants to get away from you and your misery faster than you know."*

She slowly slid down the wall and sat down, pulling her knees up, burying her face in them. Losing Ronald's love and life was more than she could bear, much more than she could imagine going through, especially with her innocent little girl, Roseline, being rejected by him. She was supposed to be their miracle, their joy and laughter, but she's become the very essence of their love's destruction, the bitterness that has polluted their once beautiful lives.

"Mom, are you okay?" Roseline touched her mother's shoulder, smiling, and in that smile, Sophie felt the love and hope that she used to feel before Ronald's return and eventual death.

She started to smile back at Roseline, but the feeling disappeared just as fast as it had come; Sophie sneered at her, "Get away from me; it's all your fault!" She snapped, throwing a glass at her.

Roseline jumped out of the way of the glass that narrowly missed her right leg. Tears welling up in her eyes, she hugged herself, pressed her thin arms around her grumbling, empty stomach, and left for school.

Roseline had become used to her hostility; there were many days like this that she left for school beat up and without having anything to eat, and some days she woke up very early not because she had an important meeting to attend but so that she could experience some of her mother's pain. While other kids her age were enjoying parental nurturing, she was experiencing parental torturing. There was nothing like an overlooked mistake in her mother's dictionary; her left hand is faster than a speeding bullet when it comes to slapping. But to whom could she possibly turn to confess her secret pain? Surely not to her dad, who was dead, who had rejected her and never even gave her a passing glance when he was home. And not her mom, who's lost her mind, oblivious to reality, permanently drowned in her misery and whiskey, ensuring she spread that misery on everything and anything within the walls of their little house. A time or two, Roseline had begged her mother to listen, but it fell on deaf ears and earned her more trouble. All Sophie's pains were directed and projected on poor Roseline. Her mom once said to her that the worst thing that has ever happened to her was giving birth to her. Even though she had nothing to do with her mother's failed marriage, Roseline continued to nurse this negative thought that the failure was her fault, and her own feeling of rejection and worthlessness overwhelmed her heart over and over; this made her develop a negative attitude toward life, which resulted in her inability to focus on her education.

There was a day in school, during her science class, when the teacher, Mr. Jones, was teaching the students about the states of Matter. She was napping in class, and he noticed.

"Now that we have established what Matter is," said Mr. Jones, "let us look at the states of matter," he continued. "A state of matter is one of the distinct forms in which matter can exist. There are four fundamental states of matter, and these states are Solid, Liquid, Gas, and Plasma," Mr. Jones explained.

Suddenly, Roseline heard Mr. Jones call her name and ask her about what he had just explained about Matter.

Jumping from her napping mode, all she could think of was a line from the Bible story her mom once told her when she was little. So, she said, "Martha is Lazarus and Mary's sister".

The whole class burst into laughter. She had never felt more ashamed.

"Really?" Mr. Jones said, smiling mockingly with arms akimbo. I noticed you've not been paying attention since the beginning of my class, so do you want to tell me what's been going on?

It was one of the worst days of her middle school year. She was very embarrassed and felt even more worthless by the incident and as if to add salt to injury, the students nicknamed her "miss Martha".

Chapter Three

Sophie had never missed her husband more, and she hadn't gone a day without thinking about him and blaming herself since he died three years ago. If only Ronald was here; if only things had not degenerated so badly between them; if only...

"Ron, how could you do this to us? How could you so cheaply lose faith in our love? Maybe I could've tried harder; I could've fought more for us. Did I give up the fight too easily? You made it impossible to reach you, Ron. Why, my sweet darling husband, my first and only love; why? Roseline was conceived from our love; she is innocent. Why, then, must she suffer for our pains? She does not deserve it. I have done her so much evil, and I don't know how to fix it. How could God have allowed all this; how had everything gotten so bad? Too many questions and no answers." Sophie sat on the kitchen floor in her smelly nightwear, lost in thought and filled with regret, tears rolling down her cheeks. And to numb the pain, she gulped some whisky, wincing from the burn in her chest as she swallowed the liquor.

The liquor could not quench the nagging inner voice, and it continued as she remembered yesterday. When Roseline returned from school, Sophie wanted to do something nice for her, so she opened the door to welcome her and tried to hug her. Only then did Sophie realize how terribly bad things were when Roseline shrank back and stiffened in fear in her arms, and she saw clearly for herself the bruises on Roseline's face and the finger marks on her arms, which she had inflicted on her own child. The way Roseline had cowered behind the door even after the hug, despite knowing she was her mother, not a stranger, broke her heart. She could see the fear on Roseline's face. The situation had been worse than terrible, so much worse than Sophie had realized or noticed. Not only was Roseline battered, but she was also painfully thin from lack of proper feeding, and her fingers trembled. Fear reached up and grabbed Sophie by the throat.

"If things were this far gone, then what was the point of my life? "I have to be gone; I can't take it anymore," she whispered inaudibly.

"Did... did... did you... say something, mom?" Roseline stuttered; still afraid her mother might hit her.

"No... nothing," Sophie answered with a forced smile.

And the ugly, condemning voice in Sophie's head came back, *"Yes, be gone already, Sophie, drink some more, add some drugs and get your life over with quickly. Ronald will never come back to you; he is gone forever, and no one loves you; no one will miss you; you are a monster. Your daughter is afraid of you; she wants to get away from you faster than you know."*

Sophie shook the voice away, took a step closer to her daughter, looking up at her with eyes filled with pain and regret; she brushed her fingers across the bruises on her face, and then, with tears threatening to pour out, she quietly walked away from Roseline back to the kitchen floor, burying her face in her knees; she wept quietly.

But this pang of regret may be coming too late for Sophie over her ill-treatment of her only child. Roseline was now 15 years old and had grown accustomed to being abused rather than loved; she had lost all sense of how to receive love, but even worse, she had developed unshakeable doubts about Sophie and Ronald Miller being her real parents. Ronald, her supposed dad was gone forever without ever acknowledging or treating her like his child. Now, it was only her and her mother. However, her mother's constant hateful actions toward her made her finally ask herself these questions: Who are my real biological parents, and how did I come to be with this hateful mom and angry deceased dad? Roseline was already far too gone battling and struggling with depression, but she didn't know. She felt as if the weight of the whole world was upon her shoulder. She was looking for answers, but no one seemed to notice. All she wanted at this time was to unravel the mystery surrounding her life and see to the end of her childhood misery. Since she had no one to talk to about her situation, she thought of killing herself, several times. But then she met a guy named Johnny.

Johnny had just been released a couple of months ago on parole from the state prison, where he spent three years and eleven months; he had served the minimum time of his sentence, which was nevertheless a long time for a first offense. He had been caught with an extraordinarily large amount of cocaine, got prosecuted by the state, convicted in a jury trial, and sentenced to state prison in California.

Johnny was someone you could easily describe as a nice guy gone wrong; somewhere along the way, he'd opted for the low road too many times, making all the wrong choices. He was pretty educated with a master's degree in Finance; though, he achieved that feat with much financial struggle and a mean determination to succeed. He was an only child of his parents, and his father died when he was only six; he was the scion of an illustrious family from the cream of social circles in Hollywood. For years after his father's death, the family fortune began to dwindle; his mother managed to squander everything his father had worked so hard to build long before Johnny became an adult. His mother's drinking habit steadily increased over time and eventually got her to end up in an institution, where she died after six months, leaving Johnny orphaned. Once his mother died, Johnny learned to live by his wits; it was all he had, and it worked well for him; at least it got him through college.

At first, Johnny had only sold drugs to people he knew and trusted just for fun and for lack of anything else to do with his free time. But eventually, he also developed a habit of the substance; hence the sales began to support the habit and his fast-growing financial needs. He had made nearly two million dollars in one year before he got caught, but even that amount of money could not fill the enormous financial hole he had dug with the financial juggling he'd done – drugs, selling short and bad investments. He had been an investment banker for a while and got in trouble with the bank, but not enough to be prosecuted, in which case, he would have been arrested by the feds – he never was for lack of enough evidence. He covered his tracks well and managed to keep living far beyond his means to such an insane degree. He had developed such a stupendous drug habit hanging out with all the wrong people that eventually, the only way to negotiate his debt with his dealer was to deal drugs for him on a larger scale, which was working out well for him until he got caught.

Johnny was very smart, handsome, and charismatic; he had a way of charming people and making them fond of him. The first time Roseline met Johnny; she was on her way home from school. Johnny was a smart dresser; he dressed to impress, was never afraid to spend any amount of money in other to catch his 'prey', and he had a sleek, sweet tongue too. He told Roseline tall tales about how he left school to start his own business and he's looking to recruit and train young men and women who are ready to make real money and become independent business owners just like him. The thought of being on her own, having everything she could dream of, seemed like a dream come true for her. Johnny did not want to rush her; he wanted to lure her gently into trusting him completely, so every day, he would wait for her on the path she took to and from school, and walked her to and from school, Monday to Friday, filling her head with all kinds of attractive tall tales. The friendship between them grew over the weeks into a strong bond – well, a strong bond it was for Roseline that she came to rely so much on Johnny. Soon enough, her peers at school, who had noticed their daily walks, began to tease Roseline about Johnny, and some asked if he was her boyfriend, to which she often blushed and insisted he wasn't.

Roseline clung to Johnny like a rock in a storm, and he faithfully walked and talked with her every day. Roseline's life with her mom remained as bleak and gray as it had been since her father rejected her and left them. But seeing Johnny every school day and eating the snacks or fast food and drinks he brings her was enough to keep her going; it was much more than she could hope for. By now, she had gotten too attached to Johnny that Monday to Friday was no longer enough for Roseline to see Johnny; the weekends had become too long to wait to see him, she craved more time with him, and so she learnt to sneak out of the house on Saturday late afternoons when her mother was fully drunk and oblivious to happenings around her to meet Johnny at a nearby park. Being with him was like taking refuge in a safe, warm place, away from her winter-cold life; Johnny was her haven, her only semblance of acceptance. Johnny had replaced her parents, and it was all the more pleasantly surprising to her when he told her he loved her one afternoon as he was walking her back from school. He had said it like a shy, well-meaning young man – he'd said it under his breath with his eyes cast down, and she'd stopped to stare at him with a stupefied expression.

"How can you say that? Nobody has ever said that to me," she responded shyly.

Johnny seemed startled by her response; it wasn't what he had expected.

"Because I do love you," he whispered, lifting her face with his finger under her chin to look into her eyes. "I mean every word of what I just said; I love you."

"I don't know what to say; nobody has ever loved me, and I don't even know what that feels like," She replied, tears filling her eyes.

"Nobody? What about your mom? You said you live with her?" He asked, feigning ignorance, having known the truth of how her mother maltreated her, which was evident from the bruises on her arms and face; though she often tried to hide that fact, he was never fooled like she fooled everyone at her school.

Turning her face away from him, she stepped back as if to walk away. But he was not going to let her get away from him, not now when he was so close to having her all to himself.

"Did I say something wrong?" Johnny asked softly, gently turning her around to face him, frowning, wondering if he had said it wrong or at an inappropriate time.

"My mom doesn't care about me; she doesn't even know where I am right now. No one knows, and no one cares." Roseline replied with such finality in her tone, the pain in her heart evident on her face.

Roseline's response was all Johnny needed for him to know that this was the right time to leap on his prey. He pulled her into a hug, kissing the top of her head, and then, he smoothly offered to take her with him to Los Angeles, California, where his business was located, so that he could take care of her and love her the way she should be loved. And in her naivety, she hung on his every word. In her disbelief and excitement at such good fortune,

Roseline suggested they leave immediately without getting to her home first, saying that she had nothing to go home to pack nor a mother who would be sober enough to comprehend or care about whatever she could say to her. Johnny couldn't have asked for better; she made it all so much easier, and with a broad smile, he picked up her school bag with his left hand and placed his right hand around her shoulders, pulling her closer, and she went away with him that afternoon, out of town, without telling anybody.

On the long drive from Corpus Christi to LA, Roseline did not say much; Johnny did all the talking while she enjoyed the sights, savoring every moment; this was her first time leaving her hometown. They stopped for lunch along the way, and she gulped down the food so fast Johnny burst into laughter. She was too excited to get back on the road and had no patience to eat slowly. They finally arrived at his home in LA at 11:30pm local time. It was dark outside, and the premises, were dimly lit, so it was hard to see anything, but the ground looked flat, easing her fear of falling and making a fool of herself. She made it safely to the front door without incident. The house was welcoming from the open door to the narrow hallway that leads into the living room; it looked expensive. Upon the walls were varied beautiful paintings, but no photographs. The floor was an old-fashioned parquet with a blend of deep homely browns, and the walls were the greens of summer gardens meeting an off-white baseboard. A sofa and a loveseat in the living room appeared like a twirl of branches, tamed by the carpenter's hand; its grain flowed as water might in waves of comforting woodland hues. Under the lamp-shine was nature's art, something that soothed right Roseline's soul. Johnny led her into the master bedroom, and its beauty took her breath away – a room of pastels awaited her at the journey's end, a room in which her spirit, soul, and body could rest and expand. She had never seen such beauty in a single room. Surely, this bedroom was the stage for her dreams; this was a haven, she thought. That night she slept like a baby, nested in Johnny's arms; he simply kissed her forehead and let her sleep like a loved child.

Roseline woke up the following morning to even better beauty as the curtains added an orange glow to the morning light streaming into the room, illuminating the dawn like brilliant fireflies; it was a perfect sunrise. It reminded her of the times as a little girl when she sat on their porch at home, watching the tree branches sway over the golden shimmer of the sunrise. For a moment, her mind conjured the rhythmic waves of the branches, and she felt her heart beating at the same slow, peaceful pace. She took a deep breath, stretching; a new day and her new life had begun. The bedsheet felt warm beneath her as the sun flooded the room more, painting the colors anew, and she felt a little of those golden rays soak into her copper-brown skin. And then, all her senses opened to the sweet aroma of eggs, bacon, and sausage served in bed with a glass of orange juice by the handsome, attractive, smiling Johnny. Being there gave her a sense of calmness, serenity, and optimism – feelings she had not experienced since she was a child. She had done something right for once in her life, running away with Johnny, she thought as she smiled shyly at him, taking a bite of the sausage he fed her.

Everything was good, so it appeared to Roseline; it felt like paradise, and she was treated like a queen. Johnny would invite friends over to his place for a party every weekend. And on weekdays, Roseline was all alone, until Johnny got back from his business in the evening; she ate whatever she wanted while watching movies all day long. She never returned to school, nor did she ever give education even a fleeting thought. She was living the life she never dreamt possible, a life she couldn't even dare to hope for less than a year ago. At last, she felt loved and respected. Roseline stretched out on the couch with a bowl of popcorn situated on her belly, all happy and dreamy, lost in thought.

Chapter Four

Bernard Hunter was just as Johnny had always described him. He was tall, shiny dark-skinned and wealthy, and Roseline had never seen anyone so beautifully created; he looked like something out of the pages of a fashion magazine, and he was very polite and gentlemanly. Bernard had come over to the house for a business discussion with Johnny; he was Johnny's business partner. In the one year that she's been living with Johnny, no one had ever visited him at home, but Johnny said Bernard was important and hadn't come to visit because he had been out of the country for the past year. Roseline's heart beat with wild joy and pride that Johnny considered her worthy of introducing her to his important, wealthy business partner and friend. Her heart sang at the thought of how special she was to Johnny.

During his discussion with Johnny, Bernard turned to look at Roseline every now and again as if scrutinizing her. She was wearing a short, tight-fitting black dress Johnny had gifted her the previous day and asked her to wear it for him to make a good impression with his wealthy business partner. Each time he looked at her, she had to smile at him, but he did not return her smile, which began to make her uncomfortable, and she would tug at her dress to force it to cover more skin. Why didn't he smile back at her? Was she looking stupid? Did he not approve of her for Johnny? Maybe he thought she was too young for Johnny, but the make-up Johnny had given and taught her to wear made her look a bit older than her age. All kinds of questions were racing through her head until Johnny's voice broke into her thoughts.

"Roseline is beautiful. Isn't she, Ben?" Johnny asked, smiling as he kissed Roseline on the forehead.

Bernard looked at her strangely with his dark eyes, scrutinizing her like a piece of artwork for purchase. Bernard stared down at her, his mouth pressed tight, and studied her silently for a while. She stood as still as she could manage under the uncomfortable scrutiny. She wanted him to think she was beautiful and approve of her for Johnny. Bernard's approval mattered to her, seeing he was important to Johnny, and she gazed up at him hopefully.

"Yes, she is indeed beautiful," he finally replied and flashed her a toothy smile.

"Thank you, Mr. Hunter; you are very kind," Roseline said, relief all over her face as she relaxed.

"Oh, please, call me Bernard, and you're welcome, Roseline," he said, smiling broadly. "I have to leave now; I will see you two soon again," he continued as he walked towards the front door with Johnny in tow.

A few days later, on September 20th, she turned 16, and Johnny invited some friends over to celebrate her sweet 16th birthday. It was her first time celebrating anything that she could remember, and it was quite an experience. Later that night, while the party was in full swing and most of their guests were either drunk or high as a kite, she had tried severally to ward off the men trying to touch her in all the wrong places but couldn't get them to stop, and she eventually ran off to find Johnny to rescue her from them. When she found him, he did nothing to make the men stop; instead, she learnt that the whole celebration was to welcome her to her new assignment.

"You have come of age, Roseline; it's time for you to start helping out around here. And you know, you got no skills, but luckily, you got something they all want, something Bernard wants and must get first; he's waiting downstairs," Johnny said, stroking her cheek gently with his forefinger and a look in his eyes that scared her.

"Wh...wh...what do you mean?" She stammered fearfully, barely audible enough.

"You're a smart girl; you'll figure it out. No rush, enjoy your party, darling," he sneered, winking at her, and walked over to a girl with barely any clothes on and started kissing her.

Roseline's heart dropped, and her stomach clenched tight as she realized she had made the worst mistake of her life in running away with Johnny. He was a devil in disguise; he was a pimp who used innocent young girls for his gain. Bernard Hunter was his client; no, not client – he was the man Johnny dealt drugs for and owed way too much money before he went to prison – Johnny's life and freedom depended on this man. Bernard was not his business partner, and their meeting a few nights ago in the house was to negotiate for her body – he had traded her to Bernard for only God knows how much and how long. Bernard was an evil gentleman, and Johnny was a liar! Johnny owned no corporate business in LA; he had lied to her. The shock made heat pour into her face and then recede in the wake of cold pain and rejection. She slowly stepped back, wanting to run as far away as possible from him, then looked up at him as he hugged the girl tightly, searching for anything that might give her an indication of why he'd chosen to discard her this way after giving her a blissful, absolutely loving one year of her life, but all she saw was mockery and bone-chilling coldness as he raised his head for a passing glance at her.

As soon as the party was over, Johnny moved Roseline to her new room, which was one of the rooms in the basement with no windows and no access to the outside world. The only access she would have to the outside world henceforth was with Johnny's clients. That much Johnny had made clear to her. Bernard was waiting in the room when Johnny led her in and walked away, shutting the door after him to give them privacy. Bernard strolled around Roseline, perusing her, then chucked her chin and stroked her cheek.

"Lovely eyes and hair like an angel," he said, running his fingers through her long jet-black hair.

Roseline stiffened. She wished Bernard would leave her alone, but he kept stroking her hair and cheek. She wanted to get as far away as she could from him with his dark eyes and mean grin.

"Please, don't do this; I love Johnny, and he loves me," she whispered, sounding stupid at the last sentence, even to herself.

He laughed. "You believe that you'll believe anything," his deep booming laugh reverberated around the room.

"Please, don't..." Roseline begged, still as a statue and eyes filling up with tears.

"Com'on; I'm harmless. Drink this; it will help you relax," he handed her a glass of whisky.

She hesitated, looking at the golden-brown liquid in the glass and had a flashback of how her mom often numbed her pain and wasted her days with the same liquid, and the tears rolled down her cheeks. For some strange reason, Johnny had never given her any alcoholic drink.

"Drink up!" He commanded impatiently.

And she took a gulp and swallowed hard, pressing her hand against her chest at the burn from the whiskey as she grimaced.

"That's it; good girl. A little of this, and you won't be scared of nothing, ever," he laughed again when Roseline grimaced with distaste and took the empty glass from her.

Shortly after that, Roseline began to feel lightheaded, and he gently moved her toward the bed, stripping her of each piece of clothing as he pushed her onto the bed. Bernard took hold of her and kissed her roughly; Roseline struggled, trying to pull away from under him, but he pinned her tightly; he was too strong for her. When she finally relaxed against him, he sexually molested her with such force and cruelty, she screamed in pain. He seemed to have been triggered by her pain as a wide, mischievous grin appeared on his face, and he continued excitedly as she clenched her fist and teeth tightly to avoid crying out any more. She had no idea how many times he molested her that night before he finally became exhausted, dressed up and left without a word, slamming shut the door after him like she was nothing.

That night, right after Bernard left her, the other men at the party took turns with her, one after the other, until she passed out. Roseline's head ached when she awakened late in the morning. The different men had given her too much to drink to relax her; her tongue felt swollen, and her whole body ached. She searched the bedside drawer and found some pain medicine, not caring if it was expired or not, she went back to the bathroom, got some water, and swallowed two tablets. She wasn't going to worry about the expiration. After last night, how could she deny God had created her for rejection, pain, and abuse? This was her lot in life. If her own mother and father could reject and abuse her, who wouldn't? Rising, she staggered into the small bathroom attached to her room, splashed some water on her face, and put on the robe she found. She staggered back into the room and tried to open the door, but it was locked; she tried again and again, and it was still locked. Then, the cold hands of fear took hold of her, and she began to scream, but none came to her rescue – not Johnny, not anyone. It finally dawned on her that she was now Johnny's prisoner, and maybe, she had been his prisoner all along and just didn't know it as she had never gone outside the house without him.

This was now her life. It wasn't something to be proud of, having multiple men of all ages in a day; some were as old as her parents. But what choice did she have? She was Johnny's prisoner; after all, it was her choice to run away with him. In her dimly lit room, Roseline sat cross-legged on her bed, clutching a green satin pillow against her chest; she fought the tears spilling down her cheeks. Why did her father hate her so much to reject her? Why did her mother always have to make her feel everything was always her fault? Why did her mother deny her any love and mistreated her? No matter how hard she tried or how well she did, it was never enough. One mistake or one thought out of line with what her mother wanted, and Roseline knew she would be told again how ungrateful, unwanted, and useless she was. And when words didn't prove hurtful enough, the slaps, kicks, and item-throws descended. Her mother never looked for her since she ran away; she had often looked out to see if there might be a report in the news of her missing, but nothing like that. It must be good riddance to this bad rubbish for her mother, who must be soaking herself in bottles of whisky while sitting on the kitchen floor or the living room floor.

"Mom wasn't wrong about one thing; it's all my fault," Roseline thought, feeling hopeless as she wept.

"Why was my mom so mean to me; wasn't a mother always supposed to love her child no matter what? Dear Lord Jesus, I have never called on you; I don't even know you like that except for what I was taught in Sunday school that long time ago when I was just a little girl and mom used to take me to Church, but I know you are up there somewhere, and you see everything. You know I loved my mother; I tried to please her, but nothing was ever enough; I was never enough for her. I ran away with Johnny to ease the burden I had become on her and make her happy. And I thought I would be free, but here

I am in a worse prison. When will this cycle of hate stop; when does it get to end?" She wept bitter tears at the cruelty meted out to her most of her life. She'd wept every night since that terrible night of her 16th birthday, hoping one day something would get her out of Johnny's prison.

"I never want to be like my mom, so help me, Lord. But I'm beginning to hate her. I had hoped to get a college degree someday, move out of the house, and be on my own, but it's as though she has her far-reaching claws of hate and rejection sunk into me to continue to perpetuate her evil through anyone wherever I go. Johnny loved me but now hates and rejects me." Roseline continued in her reflections as the tears stopped flowing.

Every which way Roseline turned, she felt trapped. There was no reasoning with Johnny; his fire was burning, and his iron-clad ego red-hot, but it wasn't anything good that Johnny wanted to have branded into her body; it was "Johnny's property", he wanted on her, for the world to know she was his to use and abuse as he wished. And he had greater plans for her; he was preparing to launch his next agenda for her.

This afternoon, she was very tired, still trying to get herself together after being mistreated by an abusive customer when she heard the stairs creak and knew Johnny was coming down. She relaxed and pressed the warming compress over her eyes; he had given her the compress for her eyes because it was often swollen from much crying. Her door swung open, and Johnny waltzed in to tell her to freshen up because he had two more clients waiting to be served as if she were a waitress waiting to take their orders for food and drinks. She made to complain but thought better of it and stared at him with disdain.

"Your job is to make them happy; you will do just that, and I'll take care of you", he yelled, noticing her disdain for him.

Johnny was high and rambling on, yelling about hating his mom for destroying his life and all his father had built. He wanted to vent his spleen on Roseline, scared she backed up against the wall.

"I'm going to tell you some real truth, so you better listen, girl!" He barked in her face, scaring her even more.

Roseline swallowed down the fear and tears to appear strong in the face of her abuser.

"All you women want to do is pretend to love someone and destroy him; you tear hearts to shreds without a thought."

He poured some white substance onto the back of his hand and sniffed it up, and his voice slurred, "None of them cares. Look at your mama; does she care about you? No!"

Roseline pressed frantically against the wall, shaking. She didn't want to hear the awful truth. Furious, Johnny pulled her off the wall to himself. When she scrambled away, he grabbed her by her hair and pulled her back. She screamed in pain and begged for him to let go of her hair. He let go of her hair, grabbed her shoulders, and shook her violently, "Sit down and listen to me," he thundered.

Roseline sat by the edge of the bed, his hands still grabbing her shoulders, and she turned her face away from him.

"Look at me!" Johnny raged, not satisfied until she obeyed.

Roseline stared at him with wide, frightened eyes, trembling violently.

"I am going to take care of you; I'm going to tell you the raw truth, so you listen and learn." He let go of her shoulders, and she sat very still like an obedient little girl.

Glaring at her, Johnny dropped into the lone sofa opposite her and sniffed some more of the white powdery substance, and threw his head back against the chair, taking a deep breath. Then, he pointed, trying to steady his hand, "Your mama doesn't care about you; my mama doesn't care about me either; she took everything from me while I was still too young to take what's rightfully mine, squandered it all and then left me homeless, desolate, and hungry. Look at you; your mama treated you worse than a filthy rag; she loathes you and rejected you. She never even looked for you for a second since you left home with a man you know nothing about. But again, you left with me because, like our mothers, you were only thinking of 'your needs' being met using me. You women are selfish! You don't do nothing for me; I do everything for you."

"No, Johnny, that's not true; I..." She stopped mid-sentence as he yelled for her to shut up, launching at her.

Roseline inched back until she was pressed tightly against the bed as though it would protect her. Nothing protected a girl from the cold hands of this scary Johnny and the harsh truth he was throwing at her about her mother. Johnny gave a sad laugh, shook his head, and sat back on the chair.

The fountain of tears finally gave way as his cruel words dug their sharp fangs deep into her fragile heart; her shoulders heaved as she wept uncontrollably.

"You're such a sweet, stupid fool," he said softly as he moved over to her side and held her in his arms. "Don't worry; I have some *'candy'* that would help you," he added.

Candy was Johnny's slang for drug, but Roseline didn't realize that immediately until he tossed her the small packet with the white powdery substance he'd been sniffing. It was cocaine.

"Put some at the back of your palm and sniff; it will boost your mood and energy, if you know what I mean. Do it now." He ordered gently.

And when she wouldn't do it, he took it from her, poured some of it into the palm of his left hand, forced her head into his palm and made her sniff it up. And that's how she was forced into using drugs. For Johnny, Roseline was his toy that he could use and control as he pleased.

Chapter Five

Roseline woke with a start in the early morning hours, all sweaty and in desperate need of a fix. The room was pitch dark; she lay dazed with a momentary loss of her sense of bearing, afraid and wondering where she was, and then, it all came back to her; she was in her prison room in the basement of Johnny's house. She propped herself up on her left elbow, rubbed her eyes with the right to adjust to the darkness and then flicked on the bedside lamp, searching for her fix. She found some poured out on the bedside drawer, sniffed it all up and laid back on the bed to savor it; she began to feel much better after a while and sat up, looking around the room. Her eyes fell on Johnny asleep on the lone sofa in her room, but unsure of whom she was seeing, she shook her head vigorously, rubbing her eyes with both hands, thinking the drug was making her see things that weren't there, and then, she whispered his name. He opened his eyes briefly, muttered something she couldn't make out and shut his eyes again. It was Johnny! At that moment, a wave of emotions swept through her – anger, pain, betrayal, but the most potent one was the urge to kill him right there.

She slowly sat up straight on her bed and allowed the thought of killing him to linger, smiling, hoping it would give her the peace and joy she craved. But the idea didn't give her peace; it troubled her heart and scared her. And for some reason, she thought it was Sunday and felt a sudden hunger to go to Church or to speak to a pastor. She didn't realize it was a weekday until she looked up at the fancy wall clock with the date; it was 2:00am, Monday, the 20th of August, one month shy of three years since that fateful 16th birthday party. She'd been in this hellhole for almost three years, and he put her in it for no justifiable reason; she'd loved Johnny and believed he'd felt the same about her too. How wouldn't she believe he did? After all, he'd treated her like a princess, like she mattered, until that night at her party. She looked at him again with a wave of burning anger. But then she questioned, did he really put her in this hellhole of a life? No, her mom set it in motion; her mom had created the hellhole and lit the fire; Johnny only helped fan the flames to keep it burning.

As she sat there thinking, all she knew was that she wanted to go to Church but knew she couldn't. She couldn't leave this room, let alone the house. Johnny finally woke up and asked what she was staring at or thinking about. There was silence between them; then, after a while, she told him she needed to go to Church, and he thought about it for a minute and asked her if she would like to see a priest. It even sounded strange to her; then, he began to laugh at the thought of her going to Church.

"Get off your high horse, girl; junkies don't go to Church. Here, take some more," Johnny said mockingly, tossing her a small packet of cocaine.

Her eyes brightened with a child-like smile, and she started to open the packet but stopped herself as the urge to go to Church enveloped her, and this time the desire was much stronger. She knew she wanted to see a pastor now. She wanted someone to talk to, someone to pray with her, as she had no idea how to pray for herself. But she felt ashamed thinking about God, especially in this room where men took turns sharing her bed. As many as six or seven men used her body in whatever way they wished in this same room in shifts in any twenty-four-hour period. She felt too filthy to call on a God so holy and pure; He was too holy to care about someone like her. And with that feeling of filthiness and shame, she gave up the idea and delved into the fix Johnny gave her. With the drug seeping into her system, she began to relax and swoon, and then that little calm voice that always seemed to show up when she least expected it came knocking in her head.

"Your mistakes do not define you; they only have a hold over you because you embrace them. People face terrible trials sometimes, things that they think will break their spirit and kill them, but they are stronger in the end for it. These trials seem like the cruelest blows when you are going through them, but strangely, they help you become stronger and better if you allow the lessons they bring to get through to you instead of the pain they inject. The pain blinds, but the lessons, if learned, enrich your life. You know, God said you would have troubles, but He will be in it with you

to ensure you come out safe on the bright side. I know this must sound crazy to you, but that's the truth. If God didn't love you and believe in you, He wouldn't give you challenges like this; your mistakes and shame are opportunities for His grace. Give Him a chance; let Him in."

Roseline smiled wistfully and shook her head. "No, I can't", she whispered. And then, getting agitated, she blocked her ears with both hands and screamed, "No, leave me alone!"

The loudness of her scream scared Johnny so much that he jumped and fell off the sofa, wide-eyed. "Stupid junkie, what's wrong with you scaring me like that? Give me that!" He yelled, snatched away the remaining fix from her, and walked out of the room, still scared, hurriedly locking the door behind him like she was a threat to his life.

She smiled slightly at the way he scurried off the room in fear; it felt good seeing Johnny so scared.

The room became as silent as a graveyard; she laid down and curled up on her bed like a foetus, her hands still over her ears; she began to cry quietly. Then the calm voice came again.

"Look at Jesus on the cross. Think of the challenge, pain, and shame that cross must have been for Him. The agony of betrayal and rejection by people He had trusted, and the death He had to accept for offenses He did not commit. But after that came His resurrection, and He proved that no challenge, not pain, not filth, not shame, not betrayal, no matter how great, not even death, could end His love for you. He had to fight death and defeat it to rise because of you – He loves you way too much to stay dead. He loves you more than you know, even in this situation. Believe and accept His love for you."

"I do not even know how to receive love, for I do not know what love is or what love looks like. I thought Johnny loved me; I accepted his love, believing he loved me, but I was so, so wrong. If only my mom had taught me what love is, who knows, my life may have turned out differently. 'If only' – that's all I have to my existence now." Roseline heard herself whispering, which made her question her sanity, and she thought the drug must be messing with her mind; she shook her head vigorously, making some guttural sounds.

Then, it was all quiet again as she lay still, curled up with her hands clasped between her knees, and a few minutes later, the calm voice returned, responding to her.

"God loves you without conditions, and He is your teacher and helper for a reason – to teach you things you do not know or understand and to help you receive them with a peace that passes all understanding that only He can give. No man can give you that."

She lay quietly for a long moment, struggling to shut out the calm voice in her head. And in spite of what seemed to her like the insanity of what the voice was saying to her that her pain and shame were opportunities for God's grace and that no matter how terrible her mess, God still loved her, she felt better, and she wasn't even sure why. Somehow, the calm voice calmed her, and she slept off like a baby, something she hadn't experienced since her 16th birthday night.

Roseline must have slept for more than nine hours; she did not wake until afternoon; it was already 2:15pm, and shockingly, no one had come to her room, no guests to serve, not even Johnny for a quickie – that's a first. It stayed that way until much later that evening as she sat huddled on her bed, leaning against the wall. The silence was calming but short-lived as footsteps and voices echoed in the distance above her, and she gulped. Then, pushing herself off the bed, she yanked on the covers, straightened the sheets, brushed her teeth, and tidied herself, spraying some perfume on herself. The bed had to be neat, and she also had to be tidy and smell good for her guests, or Johnny would starve her of food, drug, drinks, and anything else she needed as punishment. She didn't want to think about the terrible things he could do to her; the thought made her sick.

Dwayne was her first guest for the day; she'd never met him before this day. Johnny opened the door to let him in and stared at her strangely before leaving them alone; he must still be suffering from the scare she gave him earlier in the early hours. Dwayne was different; he wasn't rude and disrespectful to her like she was accustomed to with the others. He was going to take her body, and whether or not she wanted him didn't matter, but at least he was gentle and kind to her and appeared to be in no hurry to touch her. Her session with him went better than she had expected; they had more conversation than anything else. They talked about everything and anything else except her troubles and the truth about how she ended up where she was serving guests like him. She had the uncomfortable feeling that the things she had said rarely made any sense, but at least she had kept his attention. And though the blanket of deep sadness still draped around her, she could somehow sense a ray of light as she talked with him. More than once during their conversation, Roseline was almost sure the light was coming from Dwayne. They had sat on her bed talking for over an hour, and he'd still made no move to touch her. She looked at him strangely, wondering what he really wanted with her; it couldn't be that he just wanted company or someone to talk with because if that's the case, then he was in the wrong place with the wrong girl. She was only good for serving men's sexual needs and taking their brutal abuse. But after two hours, Dwayne left without touching her and gave her the most beautiful smile she had ever seen with a kiss on her forehead. If her life was a ball of a tangled mess, Roseline believed, after this experience, that Dwayne was the one who had the patience to untangle it. After he left, she felt more hope than she ever had in the last three years of her life. Though she had battled her unseen demons for so long, she had a sense of urgency and excitement about meeting Dwayne. However, she also couldn't help feeling sad at the thought that this was exactly how Johnny had been with her at the beginning before he became this monster. Was she being naive and stupid again? She'd thought as deep sadness loomed over her. She wished this would be different; she was just a girl looking to be loved and accepted.

Roseline did not see Dwayne again after that day, and each time her door opened, she jumped, hoping to see him, but no; it was always an unruly abuser. She must stay strong and keep going, so whenever her mind was tempted to imagine Dwyane and the warmth of his smile, the security of his occasional touches, she forced herself to think of Johnny's meanness or anything else that would distract her. The concentration it took to think outside of Dwayne and the false hope he'd brought her often left her exhausted, so she drowned herself in more drugs and drinks as Johnny supplied them.

Then, the gentle knock on her door came three weeks later, and she sat up straight, wondering; no one ever knocked on her door, and she didn't hear Johnny unlock the door, nor did she hear any footsteps come down the stairs or in the living area above her; she must have been zoned out. The gentle knock came again, and when she did not answer, Dwayne opened the door and stepped in, smiling. She simply smiled back to avoid Johnny's anger, in case he told him, but made no move to get up from her bed as much as she wanted to jump on him with excitement. The silence was awkward for him, and he cleared his throat.

"How have you been?"

"I'm doing good, thank you for asking. How about yourself?" She answered straight-faced without looking at him, working hard to control her excitement.

"I'm good. I've been out of town on business," he said, hoping for some friendly reaction from her.

The kindness in his voice worked warmth through her, and she looked up at him and smiled, patting the left side of her bed for him to sit down. He sat beside her, and they both sat quietly, not saying much, and occasionally stroked her cheek and kissed her lips lightly. This was all he did for two hours again; even when she'd offered her body, he'd told her he was in no hurry for that. She was even more confused this time; he was such an enigma. He left, promising to see her the next day, but she didn't believe him knowing how it played out the last time, and she bid him goodbye.

Surprisingly, Dwayne returned late in the evening the next day, letting her know he was spending the whole night with her. She had mixed emotions – joy and uncertainty flooded her all at once. But her only choice was to accept his decision because he had paid Johnny for the whole night with her. She felt joy because no other guests would come to toy with her body. And uncertainty because she did not know what to expect from him, and it scared her. She stood on her feet, a bit shaky and stared at him sadly, opening and shutting her mouth, unsure if to say something or not.

"What is it?" His words did not come out in a hurry; they did not demand an explanation; instead, his words were gentle, carefully prodding, as though he was sincerely concerned about her.

Tears flooded Roseline's eyes, and she blinked them back, struggling to speak. "I... I want to... I..." She couldn't finish, and a sense of panic welled up in her as she thought about asking him to help her get away from Johnny. What if he told Johnny and got her in trouble? What if he was a trap sent to test her loyalty? She couldn't endure any more of Johnny's punishments if he found her disloyal.

Dwayne stood watching her, confused about what to do and waited. "Take your time, Roseline. Whenever you're ready to speak, I'll be here."

Shocked at his patience and kindness to her, she looked up at him with tear-filled eyes. By the look on his face, he appeared genuinely interested in her; maybe he wanted to keep her strictly for himself alone until he got tired of her, just like Johnny did after one year. No one had ever loved her, and no one ever will – this was her lot in life. At that moment, she decided to play along with him and use that to her advantage. This was her opportunity to get away from Johnny. She stood staring at him, saying nothing with lips quivering as the thoughts ran through her mind. She had a feeling he would be content to wait like that into the night if necessary. After all, neither of them was going anywhere. Then, she exhaled slowly.

"I feel like a prisoner here; I don't get to go anywhere outside of this house, and I would like to go out somewhere sometimes... with you, if you don't mind, that is," she said, her heart beating so fast, it felt like it would burst through her chest.

"You don't go out at all? Why?" Johnny seems like a pretty great guy; I can talk to him to let you go out more often."

"No...no, no." She snapped, stuttering as she became agitated, then caught herself and calmed down. "I don't want you to talk to Johnny about this; it would appear like I'm ungrateful, and that could make him sad. Johnny does so much for me and works so hard to take care of me; I would hate to bother him with this. Besides, Johnny isn't comfortable with me going out alone because someone once tried to hurt me out there," She lied.

"Hmmm... okay," he said, nodding thoughtfully, arms folded across his chest.

"So, I would appreciate it if we could keep this conversation between us. And maybe you could work out a way to take me to lunch, dinner, or even a drive." She looked up at him, and again, she saw that strange, comforting light in his eyes. She shifted her gaze to the floor. "Please, can you do that for me?" She pleaded softly.

"I would love to take you out, but I don't know how without asking Johnny's permission," he replied warmly, which gave her more courage to push further.

"I know; you're right. Well, how about you come back for another full night and show up all dressed in a fancy suit and tell Johnny you want me to accompany you to dinner and you would have me back before 10:00 pm? But I can understand if you can't or don't want to do it; you don't like me as much as I like you. I fell for you from the first day I met you." She said, playing on his emotions.

"Yeah; I could try that, or I would figure out something better," he thoughtfully agreed, flashing her a toothy smile.

Roseline felt relieved as it appeared she'd managed to convince him that she was in love with him even though she was only looking for a way out. She was giddy with excitement but unknown to him, it was only at the prospect of freedom from Johnny and his cohorts.

Dwayne believed her easily because he was a broken man, rejected and abandoned one time too many by his ex-wife, who'd left him for his best friend. Dwayne was a man looking to be loved and accepted, desperate for approval. And it appeared to him that this vulnerable, broken woman, Roseline, accepted him wholeheartedly as he was and craved his company. No woman had ever desired his company; even with his ex-wife, he'd always had to grovel for her to go out in public with him. He wasn't an attractive man by any stretch of the imagination; he was called ugly by his parents, siblings, family, friends, and foe, all his life, and he believed it, but he was kind, generous, and hardworking. Sadly, only a few people appreciated these inner qualities without the accompanying physical beauty or attractive physical features. And he was not ready to give up on finding love; he was willing to take his chances to find love and be approved. So, if a beautiful, young damsel like Roseline, albeit used and abused, was saying these golden words to him, then he was all in and would move mountains to go out with her in public and proudly show her off to the world.

After waiting for several weeks with nothing, Roseline almost gave up hope, then Dwayne devised a plan with some of his family members from out of town, whom he paid to pretend to be high-profile business associates, and they organized a business dinner. One of them would need a beautiful escort to the dinner event, so Dwayne told Johnny about it and the large sum of money his business associate was offering for the girl who could go to the dinner event with him. Johnny's eyes lit up with greed and excitement at the amount of money to be paid for just a dinner date, and he pleaded that Dwayne put in a word for him so that Roseline could be the escort. Dwayne didn't expect it would be this easy, but when God favors you, all things fall in place for your good. Dwayne didn't have to do a thing extra to get Roseline out of the house; Johnny offered her all by himself. So, of course, Johnny got the deal and was well-paid with extra money to get Roseline a beautiful evening gown, good make-up, and a hairstylist. It cost Dwayne a lot, but as far as he was concerned, Roseline was worth it.

On the day of the planned event, 7:30pm, Roseline sat at the table with Dwayne and his pretend-business associates, eating with no idea how to get away from them without suspicion. But it would appear God's favor had the sights trained on her again, putting things in motion for her. The waitress serving their table had just arrived with their drinks; standing beside Roseline, about to serve them, someone bumped right into her, knocking the tray off her hands, and a glass of red wine Dwayne had ordered for himself tumbled down over Roseline's head, leaving dull red patches on her silver-colored dress. Dwayne rushed to her side as she frantically tried to clean the drink off her face and hair with the table napkins, and he tried to salvage her dress, but the stains weren't coming off. The young waitress, whose shirt was also drenched in drinks, kept apologizing, tears rolling down her face. Roseline, moved by her tears as she could relate to the fear the young girl was experiencing, hugged her, and told her not to worry about it. Noticing Roseline was calm, Dwayne suggested she go to the bathroom to try to use some water to clean up her dress and fix her hair. He couldn't let this mishap ruin the evening for him. Roseline nodded and smiled at him as she realized that a way of escape had just been made for her using this accident.

And that calm voice in her head whispered, *"Your challenges are opportunities for God's grace, and He will always make a way for you because*

He loves you too much to leave you in your mess."

"I guess this mishap is, but not so fast; I'm still here, and I don't know how or if I can get away without being noticed; it's just a bathroom," she muttered under her breath as she walked towards the bathroom the waitress pointed out to her.

The bathroom was right by the back door leading to the backyard, where the trash cans were stowed away. The back door was marked "Staff Only", which meant only the staff was allowed to use it. She waited patiently by the bathroom door, peeping to see if anyone would open the back door. Again, God's favor smiled on her; the same waitress who had spilt drinks on her had just ended her shift and left through the back door. The door was automated, so while it was still pulling close, after the waitress was gone, Roseline dashed through the door before it completely closed. It was pitch dark outside, and the street lights were dim. Standing outside in the face of freedom, she felt a tinge of sadness that she had to do this to Dwayne; he didn't deserve it. Or maybe all men deserved it for what they had done to her. Nonetheless, she felt bad for him; he was very kind and generous to her, but she must do what she had to do.

"Goodbye, Dwayne and thank you for everything. Another day, another time, I may have fallen in love with you. If only things were different," she whispered sadly and blew a kiss in the direction of their table.

She turned to the road and saw the tail lights of the waitress' car pull further into the distance, and she took off her heels, placing her feet on the cold dirty ground, she pulled up the long evening gown to her thighs, held it in place with her underwear, and looking around to ensure no one saw her, she bolted as fast as her legs could carry her into the pitch black, cold November night, embracing freedom with every stride, having no idea where she was headed after three years of being in Johnny's prison with hard labor.

Chapter Six

Despite the chill in the air that November night, Roseline kept going; she couldn't stop; it was not the time to get tired or allow herself to give in to her body's extreme cravings for a fix. She knew Dwayne and everyone else would be looking for her by now, and he must have called Johnny already since she's been gone for several hours; this was the point of no return. Her consolation was that Johnny would never reach out to the police in search of her because then, he would have much explaining to do concerning her if they found her before him, and he was out on parole; he wouldn't want to risk going back to jail. But she was getting more tired with stiff, achy feet, shivering, and scratching her body so much from her drug cravings; she was badly in need of a fix. She had no money and nothing valuable on her to exchange for a fix. Her own body was warring against her. Did her body not want to be free from Johnny? Was it a mistake running away? She really had nowhere to go; surely, her mother would never accept her back home; that is, if she was still alive, she might have killed herself with alcohol abuse and blamed her while at it. She pushed the thought away as she began to feel sad about her mom. She didn't want to think about that and add an extra pound of sadness to her current situation.

In the distance, she saw a park well tucked in with trees and began to walk faster to reach it. She might be lucky to find a bench to lay her head and get some rest. She slowed her pace on getting to the park, still scratching, and working hard to fight the cravings; frustrated, she kicked up some fallen leaves and stopped briefly to stare into the star-lit sky.

"Are you there, God? Isn't there someone who can help me out with this? She waited, but the only sound was the rustling of leaves in the trees overhead. "Ok, I don't need a fix; I guess you're too holy to offer drugs. I will be happy to have a warm place to stay, far away from Johnny. Can you do that for me?"

There was no response, not even the calm voice that occasionally showed up in her head, but Roseline had a distinct feeling that someone had hugged her close as she felt some warmth run through her body, and a certain peace enveloped her. A hug from someone was a rare thing in her life, the only one who made any effort to hug her was herself; she would sometimes hug herself tightly in her prison room in Johnny's house and pretend that someone who loved her was hugging her. So, this hug, this feeling of being warm in the arms of someone, must have come from God, and she could really use it right now. She glanced up once more toward the sky.

"Thanks for that, God. What am I doing?" She slapped her head, laughing and wondering if she was just desperate for warmth or was actually losing her mind thanking someone she couldn't even see for something she couldn't prove.

Shaking her head and smiling at her seeming foolishness, she walked to the other side of the park, where houses lined the park with a street separating them, and there, she found a bench. It was already

2:00am; she had been walking for six hours and was too tired; her stomach grumbled from hunger; she didn't get to eat before the drinks tumbled down on her. She curled up on the bench, folding her right arm as a pillow to support her head and her left arm moving from her upper body to her legs as she struggled between waving away insects, sleep, and craving a fix.

****

Martha Raymonds had spotted Roseline and been watching her from the moment she walked into the side of the park lined with houses, wondering what was going on with such a young girl standing out in the cold park in strappy party clothes so late at night. Martha was not one to sleep early; she would often sit by her room window in her rocking chair, reading well into the wee hours of the morning. Martha was a sweet old woman; she never had any children of her own but spent her years lovingly caring for others. In each smile, she was a mother; in her thoughts and words, wisdom flowed, and that old heart of hers was the source of hope for the hurting soul. She lived her life with purpose, running a small recovery shelter for young drug addicts and the abused, which she'd done for many years at no cost to them, and she had an uncanny way of knowing how to effectively help each one, working as if she had mastery of their souls. She always sought opportunities to be a blessing to someone. And as she watched Roseline through her window, she had an unshakeable belief that this young girl curled up on the bench, itchy and restless in the cold park across the street from her, was a soul crying for help. Martha never thought of "criminal" first; she would always think of "need and helping" first with a surety that others cannot comprehend.

Watching Roseline, there was something else – a sense of danger lurking around her that Martha couldn't put her finger on but knew she needed to act fast to reach her before the break of day. She was almost sure the young girl was not only a drug addict but had been brutally abused for too long, and she was on the run from her abuser or abusers. Whatever was happening to the young girl, it had driven sleep further away from Martha's eyes and troubled her heart so much; she began to pray for God to give her easy access to Roseline's heart, for if Roseline could trust her enough to follow her, then she could help her.

On the other side of the road, in the park, Roseline continued her struggle with sleep as the cravings for a fix intensified, and the hunger pangs became excruciating; she got off the bench, clutching her stomach and doubled over, crying out loud but Martha couldn't hear her or make out what she was doing. Then, Roseline rose defiantly and started walking toward the road separating the houses from the park. If she couldn't sleep, she might as well keep walking and search for food in someone's trash as she walked along, though she doubted there were any trashes outside in this fancy neighborhood. At that moment, Martha had a desperate desire to intercept Roseline and take her in, but then she was worried the young girl could get scared at her presence at this ungodly hour and run, especially if she was running from someone. Then an idea flashed through her mind. She dropped the book in her hand, threw a blanket on her left shoulder and rushed to the kitchen; she opened the refrigerator, grabbed the leftover apple pie, poured some orange juice into a glass, and hurried to her front door. Unlatching the lock, she stepped outside, raising the apple pie and glass of orange juice to Roseline as she saw her approaching. Roseline stopped, wary of the old lady but tempted by the food as her stomach grumbled, reminding her she was in dire need of food and drink. She had not eaten anything since 11:00am the previous day; Johnny was good at starving her.

"I just want to give you some food; you must be hungry," Martha called out loud to her. And without worrying about the ramifications if she miscalculated, Martha walked toward her with the apple pie and drink.

Roseline stood shivering and staring from the food in Martha's hands to her aged face, thinking to snatch the food and run, but something about the old lady made her feel safe.

"Take, eat... " Martha smiled kindly at her as she stopped close enough to Roseline, stretching out the food to her.

Roseline took the food from her, sat by the roadside, and began to eat hurriedly, keeping her eyes on Martha.

"I have a blanket for you. I thought you might need it; it's quite cold out here," Martha bent down and placed the blanket around her shoulders without waiting for her response.

Roseline was grateful for the blanket, "Tha...tha... thanks, ma'am," she stuttered. And she got up to leave, having finished the food.

"Dear Lord, please help me reach this young one," Martha prayed silently.

And she heard the Spirit say, *"The king's heart is in the hand of the Lord, as the rivers of water: He turns it wherever He will."*

The scripture passage came to her mind; it's from Proverbs 21:1.

"Wait, don't go, please, wait. It's dangerous out there at this time; you can get some sleep on a warm bed in my house. I'm just an old lady; I can't hurt you," Martha pleaded.

Roseline stared at the ground for a moment, then looked back at Martha. The pain and fear in Roseline's eyes were raw and deep, and Martha experienced something she'd never expected to happen in the presence of Roseline – tears filled her eyes and rolled down her cheeks at the deep pain she'd seen in Roseline's eyes.

"I'm sorry about what you have been through; please, let me help you," Martha pleaded, stretching her hands out to Roseline, and a ripple of anxiety coursed through her while she waited.

Roseline swallowed back the sobs lodged in her throat and felt her knees buckle and sway under her stiff body. She could not summon the strength to run from Martha's offer of help; only a wave of tears filled her eyes and spilled onto her cheeks. Speaking was out of the question; she took a step towards Martha and stopped, trying hard to stop herself from going forward, then she scrunched up her striking features as a series of small sobs racked her body. Martha hurried to her, closing the gap and wrapped her tightly in her arms, stroking her hair gently as she sobbed.

"Thank you, Lord," Martha mouthed, looking up to the sky as tears rolled down her cheeks.

Martha stood there in the middle of the street, hugging Roseline tight for a while, letting her cry. Martha's tears were gratitude to God and compassion for the young girl. Roseline's were tears for the abuse and rejection she'd endured most of her life and for the mother who was no mother at all. Then Martha broke the embrace, gently led her into her home, settled her in the guest room, and gave her fresh warm clothes to change into while she went into the kitchen to make her some hot chocolate to help her relax and sleep. Roseline eventually fell asleep, and Martha sat in the chair opposite the bed, watching her sleep while praying for her.

At 1:00pm, Roseline roused from sleep, opening her eyes gradually; the sunlight beamed on her face, and she winced from the brightness of the sun in her eyes. She hadn't woken to sunlight for the past three years; she had forgotten what it felt like waking up to sunlight; this was strange for her. Then, suddenly, she remembered she was on the run from Johnny; she hurriedly got off the bed to leave and stopped when she saw Martha kneeling opposite her, praying. Martha stopped and looked up at her.

"Please, wait, don't leave. At least have lunch with this old lady; after that, you can decide to leave or stay," she said, smiling with a sincerity Roseline could not deny.

Roseline nodded, scratching her body, and sat back on the bed, "Lunch sounds good, and I'd be gone after; thank you, ma'am."

At lunch, Martha barely touched her food; she spent time talking to Roseline, encouraging her to let her help her check into a recovery shelter at no cost to her, where she could also get rest, talk with a counselor, and reevaluate her life.

"No! I don't want any of that!" Roseline, agitated, pushed her chair back and got up to leave, "You just want to trap me too," she accused, scratching vigorously, and sweating profusely.

"No, my child; I just want to get you professional help," Martha smiled, making no move to stop her. "You need help to become who God created you to be, not like this. His plans for you are to prosper you and not to harm you, to give you hope and a future. You are God's masterpiece, created in His image and likeness to be every bit like Him. You are created to be loved and respected, not mistreated. You only need help to walk forward in the certainty that your future is secure; let me help you."

Roseline slowly sat down, staring at nothing in particular; nobody had ever spoken such words to her before. Then, looking at her dirty fingernails and thinking about how wild she must be looking, scratching and shaking like that, the ugly, condemning voice in her head showed up.

"The old lady thinks you are crazy."

"Well, maybe I am," she thought, pressing her temples.

"Yes, you are, and nobody really wants crazy people like you around, that's why Johnny locked you up in the basement. Nobody loves you; nobody ever had and ever will, not even your own mother. This old lady wants to deceive you into believing her just like Johnny did; she's lying to you. People care only about themselves; it's everyone for themselves. Did your own mother ever care to look for you after you ran away from home? What makes you think this woman would care about you? No; she wants to trap you into her lonely life and use you to her benefit. Can't you see she is all alone and pretending to be fulfilled but she is as miserable as you? Sooner or later, she would expend her misery on you. Run now while you still can," the ugly, condemning voice pushed.

"But why God? I've tried so hard to be loved; I've done all I know to do, and it's all gone wrong. Nothing I do turns out the way I hoped; three people I loved ended up hating me – mom, dad, and Johnny. Why should I believe this old lady now; what makes her any different from them? How do I know she is telling me the truth." Roseline continued reflectively, battling within herself.

"There is only one truth – God loves you absolutely!" The little calm voice filtered in.

Roseline bit her lower lip, the tears welling up, her throat tight and hot; she drew in a shaky breath and let it out slowly.

"I can help; let me take you to the recovery shelter, please." She heard Martha say, breaking into her thoughts.

She turned away from Martha, got up and walked toward the front door; then, as if forgetting something, she turned to Martha with tear-filled eyes, "My name is Roseline; I have been rejected and abused all my life. Both my parents hated me; my dad is dead, and my mom is an alcoholic; she's probably dead too. I ran away from home in search of acceptance and love with a man who said he loved me, and I believed and loved him too. Johnny, that's his name; he held me prisoner, in his home for three years and did the worst inhuman things to me, including forcing me into taking drugs. So, yes…, help me, please…. I… I… really have nowhere to go. Take me to the recovery shelter."

Martha got up from her seat and hugged Roseline tightly. "You can call me Martha. I will be happy to help you. Thank you for giving me the opportunity. God bless your soul, dear child." Her heart breaking for Roseline.

Then, Martha broke the hug and led her to the bathroom, handing her a clean towel and a new toothbrush, encouraging her to take a shower and brush her teeth. Leaving her to shower, Martha went to her room, opened the wardrobe, pulled out one of her unworn underwear and clothes and went back to the guest room to place the clothes on the bed for Roseline to change into when she got out of the shower; she also left her some body cream, and a comb to tidy up her hair. Later that day, Martha had Roseline checked into the recovery shelter, which she discovered was called Martha's Vineyard, where she met other young ladies like herself and a brilliant counselor – a very sweet young lady called Dr. Julia Jenkins, who was especially kind to her. She stayed at Martha's Vineyard for four months because of her drug addiction problem and made fantastic progress.

However, despite her successful recovery and the love shown her by Martha, Julia, and the staff at Martha's Vineyard, she never got over the fact that she was once a drug addict, and she allowed the stigma to remain in her mind, controlling her every waking moment; therefore, she continued to regard herself as a dirty drug addict. She allowed low self-esteem to creep into her heart, so instead of being positive, she remained negative, constantly beating up herself. She convinced herself and believed her own condemnation of herself that due to her poor educational background, she could never get a decent job and that the only choice for her to earn a living was to work in an environment that only degraded her to which she had been exposed and become accustomed to. So, she went back to the streets and met with some new girlfriends who took her to their place of work – a dance club. This was no ordinary dance club, not by any stretch; it was a Strip Club, where she had to dance almost naked for every and anyone, mostly men, and they paid to watch her and, sometimes, touched her in all the wrong places; she didn't care as long as it put money in her pockets. And without a word, Roseline ran away from Martha's motherly love and influence to become a professional stripper at the club.

Chapter Seven

Easter day was unseasonably cold this April. Martha found she needed a thicker sweater when she stepped out onto the front porch and went back inside to get a throw blanket. It was a typical Easter Sunday at Martha's Vineyard – relaxed but bustling with activities. Some of the staff handed out gifts to the housemates, and others served food and drinks to everyone in the house, including the visitors. Martha loved the presence of everyone, but she needed to clear her thoughts; she couldn't stop thinking about Roseline and how she left the Vineyard without a word to anyone. She had prayed for her every day since she left a month ago, hoping she might have a change of heart and return to the Vineyard; the young girl still needed a lot of work on her heart and her fragile relationship with God. With a throw blanket around her shoulders, she closed the door behind her to shut out the noise inside and found Julia sitting alone on one of the porch chairs.

She laid a hand on Julia's shoulder. "Thank you for all you do in this place; it's a great event."

"Yeah, it's great. Thank you for making it possible, too. We couldn't pull it off without you," Julia turned smiling, her eyes veiled with sadness.

Taking a seat beside her, Martha sighed, leaned back, and fixed her gaze on the trees that lined the street. "It's Roseline, isn't it?" Without waiting for Julia's response, she continued, "It's hard to believe. She just vanished like she was never here at all."

Julia blinked back tears as she looked ahead, staring at nothing in particular, then smiled tiredly. "She still had so much to learn; I wish she had stayed; she was much loved by everyone here. Why did she leave?"

"I wish I could tell you why, but I have no idea," Martha answered sadly.

"I don't get why she chose to leave just when it mattered the most for her stay. She could've spoken to me, whatever it was. And how did I not see it? How did I miss the signs that she would run when she began to experience real love from other people because she didn't know how to receive love having been abused most of her life? I was her counselor, and I have been down this road before, so I should have seen it. How did I miss it?" Julia said, feeling frustrated.

Julia had endured much rejection and abuse. She never knew her father, and her mother, a drug addict, never wanted her and once traded her to a young man at age two for a fix; a kind neighbor had come to the rescue of the poor child, giving her mother the money that she needed to pay for the fix. And when she attempted to trade her a second time, child protection services waded in and took the child away from her, putting her up for adoption. But no one showed any interest in adopting Julia for a long time, so she had to go through the foster care system. She had gone through 14 foster homes with much physical and sexual abuse by age nine before a loving family finally adopted her, changed her life for the best, and sent her to college when it was time. After graduating from college, she met Martha, and Martha introduced her to Christ. The old lady had been like the doting grandmother to Julia since then.

"It's not your fault, Julia, don't blame yourself; you did your best for Roseline; we all did. You couldn't have stopped her. We can only pray for her now."

"I do miss her; she had become like a kid sister to me," Julia said thoughtfully.

"I miss her too. I think about her and pray for her every day. You know, sometimes, when I heard her put herself down so low with all those negative, false ideas about herself, I wanted to shake her so hard and shake out those falsies from her head to remind her she's God's masterpiece with a great future ahead," Martha smiled wistfully.

Julia kept her eyes on the horizon. "God is a good Father; He will take care of her. Roseline is His, as we are, and He loves her too much to let her waste her life. Our part is to keep knocking on heaven's door for her."

They both sat in silence for a long while, staring

into space. A breeze stirred the trees, and Martha thought about the first time she met Roseline and how far she'd come since then before she vanished, and she felt grateful for the opportunity God gave her to have been a part of Roseline's life. Roseline had recovered and made good progress on her drug addiction; she was learning the Word of God and even praying more often without being prodded. Martha inhaled long and slow and smiled, reaching to pull Julia close as she leaned her head on Martha's shoulder. "God's got her, Julia; she will be fine."

As much as possible, Martha tried to live her life without looking at the waves – she had a way of weaving scriptures into every situation. She remembered the Bible story of one of Jesus' disciples, Peter, getting out of the boat and walking on water to meet the Master. Peter walked along quite confidently until he looked at the waves and began to sink, but when he cried out for help, the Master showed up for him. So, even when she had looked at the waves when some difficult situations had caused her faith to waver a little, God showed up. God had calmed the raging sea before in the lives of many under her care; He would do it again in Roseline's. This certainty kept her eyes away from the waves to where they belonged, straight ahead to the Lord.

****

At the club's main entrance, Roseline heard the men talking about her as they tried to get in. She hurried into the club through the staff entrance, straight to the empty changing room, so they wouldn't know she'd been listening to their conversation about her from the side of the building.

So that was how these men saw her – nothing but a worthless game to satisfy their lust whenever they needed it. Roseline felt deeply hurt about being described that way, and tears flooded her eyes. But she couldn't understand why she felt so hurt; after all, she already knew this reality, and this time, she chose this lifestyle and was not forced, yet she was hurt. Fine. If that's how they saw her. Her shoulders tensed, and she grabbed a makeup wipe and wiped her face to reapply her makeup before her show started in a few minutes. She defiantly stepped out onto the dance floor and gave them her best performance, telling herself she would take her game a notch higher and satisfy their lust all right, but she would not do it worthlessly; she would make it worth every dollar in their wallets, and would not stop until she emptied them. And that she did, as never had she had so much money doled out to her like that night, and she felt good about it.

However, after she left the dance floor and returned to the dressing room, a pang of deep sadness and emptiness overcame her, and a hint of guilt as well for the way she left Martha's Vineyard without a word. She missed Martha, Julia, and the people at Martha's Vineyard; they had treated her like she was something special and important when she was no more than a worthless game, just as the men confirmed. Even her mother had treated her like a worthless item. Why would Martha and Julia think any different of her and treat her so good if it wasn't a trap to earn her trust first as Johnny did? Still, she missed them so much it broke her heart. Leaning forward on the dresser, staring into the mirror, she slowly sat down on one of the chairs, tears rolling down her face. She wiped the tears, wondering what was happening to her; she was used to the sadness and guilt about them, but the tears were something new. Sometimes the thought that they may have been true to her caused the guilt to grow so loud that it almost took a voice – a voice that kept her awake most days, even when she was dead tired. Hadn't she read in the bible Julia had gifted her, which she'd left behind at the Vineyard, that the Holy Spirit convicts the world of sin? This feeling of guilt, was it the conviction?

And out of nowhere, the calm voice said, *"I stand at the door of your heart, knocking... if only you will open your heart."*

The voice was not audible, but it made her wince. The same had kept her awake several times when she was supposed to be sleeping. She would often roll over, hoping for some peaceful, well-earned sleep. But the voice of guilt would show up repeatedly, persistently calling her to God's love, regardless of her lack of interest and, even worse, her lack of worth. Why would God want a worthless girl like her? Even her mother, father, Johnny, and the men didn't want her for her worthlessness; she was only a game to be used and abused as they wished. She stared at her image in the mirror and saw nothing worthy - no education, no skills. Too tired and psychologically drained for another performance, she obtained permission from the manager to leave for the night, making an excuse that she felt too ill to perform, and strode out of the club.

The night was nice and cool; Roseline decided to walk home instead of using a cab to get some air in her head; it was only a 40mins walk from the club. She shared an apartment with two other girls, who were dancers at the club and had become her friends; they were off duty tonight, and she could really use their company as she was still feeling quite sad. As she approached her street, she noticed the coffee house across the street was still open and saw her two housemates seated there. Excited, she crossed over and sashayed into the coffee house, loudly greeting and high fiving her friends before settling down to order a cup of coffee.

Her friends were nothing like Martha, Julia, and the family at Martha's Vineyard – they were not godly and loving, but they were loyal. And they didn't expect from her anything that she wasn't willing to give, nor tried to push her to believe what she couldn't think about herself; they accepted her just as she was. There was Melody, the Caribbean girl who dreamed and constantly talked about getting to New York and playing the violin for a Broadway orchestra, and there was Ama, a petite Texan girl who had been dreaming for years of getting herself into an Ivy League college to study medicine and travel to Africa. They were both girls with dreams in their eyes and never judged Roseline for not having any dreams to look forward to her future. Thus, the three of them fit well together. However, beyond their shared lifestyle, they had something more significant in common - their discontentment with life and the abuse they had all endured.

Melody was twenty-two and had been beaten by her ex-husband into a coma, which she survived after six weeks. Ama was twenty-one years, kidnapped at the age of four and lived with her kidnapper, who was 38 years older and sexually abused her for 15 years before she found a way to escape a little over a year ago. She had no recollection of her parents or if they were still alive.

"I should be practicing right now; I will never make it into a Broadway orchestra if I spend all evening here listening to y'all and other people's music," Melody laughed.

Then, Melody launched into a description of some Broadway musicals she had seen in the past, and Ama was immediately caught up in the conversation, trading opinions, albeit meaningless, to keep the excitement going, but Roseline was not in the mood for that; she'd heard the same Broadway stories a million times from Melody. Normally, an evening like this, hanging out with her two friends, would leave her feeling like she could conquer the world, but tonight was different. The feeling of emptiness and sadness was back again; she felt as if something was missing from her life, something she couldn't describe or put her finger on. It was deep, far down inside her heart, like a bottomless hole that nothing could fill.

"You ok, Rosie?" There was a break in the conversation; Ama touched her hand, her forehead wrinkled in concern. "You don't seem like yourself tonight."

Roseline shrugged, "I just don't feel good."

Melody, concerned, leaned back in her chair, her head angled curiously, "You haven't been sleeping well lately. What's going on, did one of those men at the club hurt you?

"No, nothing like that; I guess I'm just tired. Dancing to please others can be physically draining. I have to leave you, ladies; I will go to the apartment and get some rest."

"Ok, dear; we'll see you later," Ama said, got up and hugged her.

Roseline stepped out of the coffee house with a feeling of uneasiness she couldn't explain; she looked around, and the street appeared the same as usual, nothing out of place. Since running away from Johnny, she'd made a habit of always watching over her shoulder. And with all appearing clear, she stepped onto the street and started walking home. She didn't realize she was being followed and never knew someone had been stalking her for days. Just as she entered her house ready to close the door, she felt a much stronger force from the outside push the door back at her, throwing her to the ground.

It was Johnny! This was her worst nightmare.

"How did you know my house? Who gave you my address?" She asked, scared, and crawling away from him.

"You think you can hide from me?" Johnny barked, laughing wickedly. "It's me, Johnny. I have eyes and ears all over."

"What else do you want from me?" She asked, her voice shaky, with fear written all over her face, "I trusted you with my life and followed you to this state without the knowledge of my mother, and you ruined it for me… "

Before she could say any more words, Johnny slapped so hard across the face, her head spun, and she screamed as he slammed shut the front door, drowning out her scream.

"I knew sooner or later we would meet again," he bent over her grinning viciously.

Then, he caught hold of her and dragged her to the bathroom. Kicking and scratching him, she tried to get away from him, but he grabbed her head and forced it into the toilet bowl. Fighting for breath, her hands reaching for anything to grab, he stepped down hard on her hand and pushed her head harder and deeper into the bowl. Terrified by the heavy weight of his hands pressing her down, she fought. When her lungs burned for hair, and she was losing consciousness, he pulled her head up.

"Had enough water yet?" He mocked.

"Enough, please," she rasped, dragging in some air.

He shoved her head down again, flushing the toilet for more water in her face; she bucked and kicked, clawing for escape. When he pulled her up again, turning her around to face him, she choked and coughed hard, pleading for mercy. He laughed, and she knew he was enjoying the evil he was doing to her. He stood in front of her, feet planted apart and reached for her head again. An ungodly fury rose in her, and she swung her fist straight and sure at his crotch. When he dropped to his knees, groaning, she scrambled out of his reach. In his mean stubbornness, despite the pain, he went after her and caught hold of her; she screamed, kicking, scratching, and gasping with effort. He had one hand at her throat when the door burst open, and Melody and Ama stepped in. He got up so fast it was like lightning, knocking both girls out of the way and bolting away from the premises.

"What in the world was that; what happened?!" Melody exclaimed, scrambling up on her feet and catching her breath, while Ama cried out in pain about her shoulder getting knocked off the joints.

Suddenly, noticing Roseline's bad shape, both girls rushed to her side, "Are you ok? What happened? Who was that? I'm calling the police," Melody said.

"Oh no, no police, please; I will explain everything to you." Roseline panicked. And they sat holding her while she told them all about Johnny and how she'd run away from him, and she didn't know how he found her.

"If you both hadn't come in the time you did, he would've killed me; I would be dead by now," she whispered, looking up at them with gratitude.

They sat right there on the floor, where Johnny had almost strangled Roseline to death, holding her while she wept, furious that she didn't want them to call the police after Johnny and had to respect her wishes. And the three of them sat there in pulsating silence, each in her own thoughts. Roseline had seen clearly enough that something dark and evil existed inside Johnny; she recognized that menacing evil look in his eyes, and she had seen it before on one other man's face – Bernard, when he'd molested her repeatedly that night of 16th birthday. She'd never thought of Johnny as capable of killing anyone, but now she'd seen the possibility in him, for he was a man controlled by the demons from hell. Helpless rage and fear feasted on her, but she knew that fear was the very last thing she could allow to take control of her; it would only cripple and eat her alive. She must find the strength to forge ahead without fear. So, help me, God; I need strength, she thought.

"The name of the Lord is a strong tower; you run to it, and you are safe," the calm voice filtered in.

You sure do have a way of showing up, Roseline thought, nodding with a sad smile playing at the corner of her mouth.

Then, Ama broke the silence, "It's dangerous for you to remain here; the bastard could come back to finish what he'd started," she said, looking at her friend with concern.

"Yes, he would surely come back; he's insatiable, but I will no longer run; I'm tired of running," Roseline replied thoughtfully. And at that, she concluded that it was time; she must put an end

113

to it all; there was nothing left for her in this cruel world. She had made up her mind long ago never to return to that life with Johnny again, and now he'd found her. But he would never own her again!

Chapter Eight

Long after Melody and Ama had gone to bed, fast asleep in their rooms, Roseline lay wide awake on her bed, lost in thought. It's early hours, the room is pale, and the soft perfume blend of orange, orchid, jasmine, water lily, rose, ylang-ylang, and musk wafted from the candle burning on her nightstand. She inhaled deeply as she sat up, pulling up her knees against her chest and pressing her head against her knees, she rocked herself back and forth, smiling cynically. She hadn't shed a single tear since she'd almost lost her life at the hands of Johnny; maybe she was still in shock. She often found some solace in crying out her pain, but the tears seemed to have deserted her as well, like everyone else who'd been in her life. So, what was the point of her life; what was the point of her still being alive? Was she alive to keep suffering and be at the mercy of others to use and abuse? That's no life. Martha would often call her God's masterpiece, but all she'd ever been was a pun in other people's cruel games. As far as she knew, masterpieces are treated with respect and care, and she had never been treated with respect or even consideration, except for Martha and Julia, but she couldn't muster the will to believe them because she always felt they were only being nice to her to suck her into their web as Johnny did; she couldn't trust them enough to believe – but that's on her. Besides, they were such opposites to her: they were whole, and she was broken. They were hopeful, but she was hopeless – she could endure her despair but not their hope for her. They were faithful, and she was faithless. They were kind and giving; she was too scared to give. They were loving, and she didn't know how to receive love because she was never taught love. And they were honest, but she lied and betrayed them when she ran away without a word. Even if she wanted to, she could never return to Martha's Vineyard; she had burnt that bridge all by herself without any help from Johnny or the devil.

Now, here she was, couldn't cry, couldn't sleep, couldn't eat, beaten, choked, strangled, and still alive. For what? She couldn't think of a single thing she could be living for. For her mom? A mean-spirited alcoholic completely focused on herself and hated her only child. For education? She couldn't keep up in any of her classes with a constantly grumbling stomach, body aches from her mother's beatings, and of course, mean kids who couldn't spare her a kind word, and now she had neither the will nor the money to go back to school. For a boyfriend? She could only laugh at herself on that one, for the one and only boyfriend she ever had – Johnny, was the universe's cruel joke on her. For work? The very people she danced to entertain saw her as nothing but a worthless game to satisfy their lust. For friends? She had not a single one she'd allowed herself to trust, not even Melody and Ama, who was as broken as her, for she couldn't let any into her heart lest they destroy what was left of it. So, there was nothing to live for and nowhere to turn. Freedom was only a figment of her imagination, a hopeless dream; she could never be free.

Roseline's head was beginning to hurt from so much thinking; she got up and stood by the window and saw the dark frame of a man strolling down the street at that ungodly hour. She waited for him to come under the light of the street lamp to see who could be roaming the streets alone at that time, but he didn't. It was a much-needed distraction, so she watched him until he sat under a small tree not too far from her building and raised his head, a little light cast on his face.

"Johnny!" She raised a trembling hand and put it against the glass; the cold seeped into her palm and up her body, leaving goosebumps all over her body. She put her hands around herself and took a step back, mouth and eyes wide open. What is he still doing here? Was he waiting for her friends to leave to finish her off? She wondered as the cold hands of fear gripped her in the throat.

"Oh God, I'm suffocating; help me," she whispered, heart pounding. She began to shake and pulled the curtain close. Maybe, this was the only way out – death. But she would not give Johnny the satisfaction of being the one to send her packing from the world.

"Fear not, child. The Lord is your present help in time of trouble," the calm voice filtered in.

"Fear not? My help in trouble?! That's all you can

say?! How present was the Lord when he almost killed me earlier?!" She yelled at the calm voice, pointing in the direction of Johnny under the tree.

Trembling, Roseline slumped to her knees, trying to calm herself not to awaken Melody and Ama. She did not want any trouble for them both with Johnny; he could hurt them if they got in his way, and they knew too much already to get them in trouble with him. This was her cross, and she must bear it alone. Why did he have to find her? She had come to accept things the way they were, and she was getting by. Why did he have to come to destroy her inner stillness? She clenched her hands into a fist as the image of him strangling her came before her again. Her only offense was being born. She knew what she had to do; it was the only way to bring all the pain to an end. She would send herself to the place where she never had to worry about freedom – a place far away from the evil world's reach. No one could ever use or hurt her if she were dead.

"This day, choose life and live; don't give up," the calm voice came again.

"No, living is pointless," she whispered.

****

On the other side of the same city, at the same hour, Martha sat by her window with a heavy heart, praying for Roseline. She could sense something was wrong with her wherever she was; the urgency in her spirit to pray for her was unsettling. Plus, the recent news reports of the rate at which young people were committing suicide and doing drugs had become alarming, and she could no longer reason away the possibility that Roseline could be in harm's way or worse. She had talked with Julia at length about it earlier and found Julia had the same concerns. They had shared a word of prayer for her, and Julia had promised to keep searching for Roseline, reaching out to more people she knew who might be able to help find her, praying she was still alive. Every night, day, and each morning since she left, Martha had prayed for Roseline, asking God to get her attention and bring her back to them, but most especially, reveal Himself to Roseline that she may live in the reality of faith in Christ and the certainty that life came from a God who unconditionally loves her, regardless of the heartaches and pain that life dealt her and what she might think of herself. Martha not only prayed every chance she had, but she fasted as well. Fasting wasn't something she often did, considering her old age, but the urgency in her spirit the past few days called for that.

"Father, let your grace and love prevail in Roseline's life; don't let her get away from you, Lord," Martha whispered, looking up to the sky from her window.

The answer she heard, deep in her soul, was the same she'd heard all day. *"The thief comes only to steal and kill and destroy; I have come that they may have life and have it in abundance."*

It was one of Martha's favorite scripture verses. Back then, when she was only a young girl, having lost her parents in a car accident that she survived, that scripture had opened the door to her blossoming understanding of all the goodness God had in store for those who followed Him. Now, it reminded her that whatever Roseline was battling would not be happening except for one thing: the enemy was at work to get her soul. She did not know what might be happening to Roseline right now, but she had a quiet assurance that no matter how bad Roseline's situation was, God would win in the end – it didn't matter what that winning might look like; His purpose would prevail. And at that, Martha sighed, walked away from the window, and went to her bed to get some sleep. But hard as she tried, she couldn't sleep, and then she was reminded of the bible verse, *"Pray without ceasing,"* - 1 Thessalonians 5:17. And she lay awake communing with the Holy Spirit silently.

Chapter Nine

In the morning, Melody and Ama hurriedly left the house for an appointment with a private client after checking on Roseline to be sure she was good, and in their rush, Ama did not pull the front door shut hard enough for it to lock properly; thus, though seemingly closed, the door was unlocked. Roseline had leaned against her room door and reassured them again that she was good, so she did not get to the front door to check it after they left. Also, in her despair, she had forgotten the maintenance man, Philip, was coming that morning to fix their kitchen sink, which was leaking. So, she wasn't expecting anyone except Johnny, whom she had seen through her window lurking around in the early hours but was no longer there or around the area as far as she could see. But that didn't matter to her anyway; she would be dead before he returned to finish what he had started the previous day. And while busy setting up her scene of departure, she did not hear the maintenance man, Philip, when he knocked, and the door slid open slightly by his third knock, which was harder than the first two knocks. He'd known the ladies since they moved into the apartment a few months ago and had helped them fix things in the place a few times and even sat to share ugly tales about the neighborhood over a cup of coffee with them. So, he was surprised they would be so careless as to leave their front door open; he pushed the door wider and poked his head into the apartment, calling out if anyone was home while also prepping for any attack, in case it was a break-in.

Rosaline stood on a dark wooden chair with a noose around her neck hanging from the ceiling fan holder; she took a deep breath and was about to kick the chair from under her feet to hang herself.

"JESUS"! Philip shouted and rushed in, grabbing onto her tightly as she struggled to be free of him, kicking and hitting him like a deranged one.

"Let me go; I have to go. Let me go, please; I'm tired

of hurting and running," Roseline cried.

"Stop it, Roseline! Do you think taking your own life will put an end to your troubles?" He shouted, holding her tightly against his broad chest with one hand and taking the noose off her neck with the other.

That word touched something in her, and she stopped fighting him but angrily retorted, "And what is that thing that will put an end to all this suffering that is tormenting my life?"

"It's not a thing; His name is Jesus," he replied, lifted her in his arms and sat her down on the chair.

"Jesus?" She hissed and laughed cynically, rolling her eyes, thinking, "yeah, right. Where was Jesus when Johnny found me and almost killed me yesterday."

Philip seemed to have understood what she was thinking laughing like that, and he quoted Isaiah 53:5, *"He was wounded for our transgressions, He was bruised for our iniquities; The chastisement for our peace was upon Him, And by His stripes, we are healed"*. He paused, then added, "Let Jesus heal your wounded heart!"

But that only angered Roseline, and unable to contain her pain, she started yelling, recounting the tale of her woes, everything she had ever been through; how she was rejected, beaten, molested, mocked, and constantly drugged, and how she couldn't bear it anymore.

"You have been through so much, Roseline, and that is why Jesus said in Matthew 11:28, *'Come to me, all of you who are weary and carry heavy burdens, and I will give you rest.'* He's been waiting to lift your burdens if only you would let Him," he added. "God heals the brokenhearted and binds up their wounds," Philip continued, quoting Psalm 147:3. "God can rescue you from the world, Roseline… if you let Him in," he said with such undeniable sincerity that it brought tears to her eyes.

This was the first time tears had come to her eyes since the attack from Johnny the previous day, and she let the dam of tears break loose as she doubled over on the floor and wept. Philip got down on his knees, gathered her in his arms, and let her cry it all out. When she had cried her fill, Philip released her, and she sat up straighter. Something was happening inside her, like sunshine warming her body, sending rays of light into the darkest places in her heart. And she began to remember the story of Apostle Paul that Pastor Trenton had shared the first time Martha and Julia took her to Church after her recovery from drug addiction. When Paul was thrown into prison, awaiting sentencing, Jesus stood up for him; He rescued him and threw the prison doors open for him. Emotion built inside her. How wonderful it must have been for Paul to know that God was on his side. What would it feel like to know God loved her? She smiled.

"Jesus died on the cross so that he could rescue you from everything in this world – from rejection, abuse, hunger, homelessness, loneliness, pain, and even death... just as he rescued me," Philip clasped his hands and leaned forward, "Because He loves you without conditions and he desires to rescue you," he added, intensely serious.

"Rescue?" The word played across her wounded heart like a soothing balm. "Rescue" – that's what she had always needed, always wanted – back then, in Johnny's basement, and even now from Johnny, from death, and much more from herself. And that was when she realized that, more than anything, she needed Jesus right now. It wasn't a promise she felt worthy of claiming, but for reasons she couldn't understand, she became calm, drawing a slow, deep breath, as the word "rescue" made her teary, and she began to nod in response.

Right there, Philip led Roseline to Christ; she surrendered her life to Jesus. He prayed and gave thanks to God for her salvation and for the privilege for him to have been in her apartment that morning.

"Do you have anyone I can call for you? I mean, I know there is Ama and Melody. But is there anyone else outside of them where you can go for a while, away from here, at least until things settle?" He asked, "And we'll report the attack from Johnny to the police; they have to find him and get him off the streets," he stated with a finality she couldn't argue.

She hesitated and then replied, "Yes. I have someone, Dr. Julia Jenkins… at Martha's Vineyard," and she gave him the phone number for Martha's Vineyard.

At the first ring, Julia hurriedly answered the phone,

as she was expecting a lead's feedback on Roseline. She had been working the phone all day, calling every possible lead she had in search of Roseline. Julia noted down the address and dashed out the door to get Roseline.

That same morning, Johnny had gotten into a fight with a drug dealer a few streets away from Roseline's, and the drug dealer had shot him point blank on the head. Johnny lay dead on the street in a pool of his own blood. The paramedics came and took his body away. Later that day, Roseline learnt of his death when Philip, Julia, and she went to report the attack at the police station. His killer had not yet been found.

A few weeks after that, Martha encouraged Roseline to reach out to her mom and make peace with her, so she travelled back to Corpus Christi, Texas with Julia and discovered her mom had committed suicide about a year ago and was buried beside her dad.

Roseline wept for Johnny and her mom, for all the wasted years and for the man and the mother they could've been if only they had made a different choice than the path they chose for the pain other people had dealt them... if only. But now, she was thankful for her second chance at life; she had her whole life ahead of her with Jesus on her side, she could handle anything.

"Let's go home, sis," she said, smiling at Julia, and hand in hand, they walked to Julia's car.

They drove back home to Los Angeles, California, where she lived with Martha, having accepted the old woman as the grandmother she never had. She had a place now she could truly call home, where she was much loved, and she had a job, working as a filing clerk at Martha's Vineyard. And since that day, Roseline felt renewed and had peace like never before. All her fears, anxieties, and negative thoughts gradually seeped away. Though thoughts of her past occasionally poked into her mind, she simply does as Apostle Paul says in Philippians 3:13 – 14 "... *forgetting those things which are behind and reaching forward to those things which are ahead. I press toward the goal for the prize of the upward call of God in Christ Jesus.*"

Roseline now 22 years old, had been living with Martha for one year now, and Martha spoilt her silly; she couldn't have asked for a better grandmother. This beautiful Saturday afternoon, Roseline's heart lifted as she sprawled on the carpeted floor in her room, reminiscing about what her life was now and what it was not too long ago. And this was only the beginning, Martha had often said to her, quoting Joel 2:25: *"And I will restore to you the years that the locust hath eaten, the cankerworm, and the caterpillar, and the palmerworm, my great army which I sent among you."* God was up to something amazing in her life; she smiled. She looked at her watch and realized she had less than an hour to get ready for their Church's singles fellowship picnic. They had agreed that Julia would pick her up from home, and they would go together.

The word "home" sounded like a dream to her but it was all real; she had a home now with people who truly loved her – *"Yes, Julia was picking her up from home,"* she smiled thoughtfully as she got up, rushed a shower and was ready before Julia arrived.

There were all kinds of fun activities lined up at the picnic, including tug-of-war, which was Julia's favorite game; they joined the Green tugger team since they both belonged to the Green singles group. Their group lined up on the left side of the referee, and the Red team lined up on the right side, with the Red team boasting about being the king of tuggers.

"You all think you the king; oh no, no, no, not this time," Julia yelled, doing her signature victory dance to the amusement of everyone, "Com'on Greeners, grab the rope and get ready to win," she added, striking a pose, while taking hold of the rope.

Both teams took their places and grabbed the rope, and a young man in the Red team stuck his head out of the line and made eye contact with Roseline and smiled. Something in his smile made her heart skip a beat, and she couldn't help but smile back at him.

"Pull!" The referee instructed loudly.

The young man, who seemed to have forgotten what he was there for, kept staring and smiling at Roseline instead of pulling the rope, and as his teammates pulled the rope, he lost his balance and was yanked forward by the Green team where he fell face flat on the ground. Julia and her teammates surged backwards in what was an unquestionable victory.

"We did it; yes!" Julia pumped her fist into the air and did more of her victory dance, pulling Roseline into the dance, but she was too shy, her eyes still on the Red team guy who fell.

Julia stopped and followed her gaze, "What are you looking at?"

"Nothing," she turned away, but it was too late; Julia had caught her.

"Hmmmm... you're looking at that guy, the one who fell," she teased her. "I think he likes you; he's been staring at you since we arrived. And he is gooooorgeous!" She whispered, winking and smiling at Roseline.

The young man dusted himself off and took a fair amount of mock jabs and teasing from his teammates before walking towards the two ladies.

Roseline turned and kept her back to her apparent admirer, and hissed in a whisper, barely loud enough for Julia to hear, "Stop staring at him; you're embarrassing us," she grabbed Julia's hand, pulling her away from there.

"Hey Ladies, please wait," the young man shouted.

And they both whirled around at the same time. His gaze connected with Roseline, and she felt an attraction that went to her very core, way beyond anything she'd ever felt.

"I'm Jim Kingston," he said confidently, stretching out his hand to Roseline for a handshake; she took his hand, and Jim held it longer than a handshake, staring and smiling at her like no one else existed around them.

Julia looked from Jim to Roseline and back again. "I'll be right back; see y'all later," she smiled knowingly and walked away, leaving them standing there.

"Oh, okay," Jim tore his eyes away from Roseline for a moment and glanced at Julia, "Nice to meet you; I didn't get your name, though," he said as she continued to walk away, smiling without a response.

Roseline tried to suppress a smile as Julia left. He noticed it, and a toothy grin spread across his face. "I wasn't trying to get her name; I was trying to get yours," he said softly, gazing at her.

She felt something inside her begin to melt under his unshakeable gaze, "Roseline... Roseline Miller... that's my name," she stuttered, unsure about adding her last name.

"That's a beautiful name; I love it," he said, taking her hand and walking her to the sitting area, and they sat there talking until his name was announced for his teaching session to begin; he got up, promising to be back.

Roseline sat there speechless with her mouth open as he walked away, smiling at her lovingly, surprised as to who he was and why such an educated, accomplished young man would be interested in an uneducated, ordinary girl like her. And when she turned and looked ahead at the sea of young heads, she saw Julia smiling mischievously at her.

Julia knew all along who he was; he hadn't been around for over a year, so Roseline couldn't have known him. Jim was the son of the Church missionaries in the Caribbeans, Evangelists Anthony and Olivia Kingston. Jim, 27 years old, was a medical doctor and a youth missionary in charge of youth outreach programs in Trinidad and Tobago; he was currently living between Trinidad and the US but was transitioning fully back to the US in a few weeks. However, he was more of a country boy and loved nature, so she doubted he would be returning to live in LA; he would probably settle on a ranch in the countryside and shuttle to LA.

"Lord, what are You up to?" Roseline whispered, looking up to the sky.

"Child, I know the plans I have for you, plans to prosper you, plans to give you hope and a future," the Holy Spirit filtered into her heart.

And a certain peace permeated her entire being. Smiling, she got up and moved closer to the front and sat beside Julia, gazing, and listening to Jim teaching this crowd of young people so boldly about Christ, and he occasionally stole glances at her, sending a smile her way every now and then.

Julia looked at her, smiled, pulled her into a side hug, and whispered, "He's a good man, and you deserve a good man, don't sell yourself short. God's only just begun with you; you are a blossoming love story of God's love for us all," she whispered as if confirming what the Holy Spirit had dropped in Roseline's heart minutes ago.

"Thank you, Lord. Indeed, you have only just begun with me. And this beautiful sister and grandmother you gave me – Julia and Martha, are a true reflection of your love for me... and, I guess, Jim too; so, I'm completely trusting you to lead me. I joyfully look forward to what you have in store there for me," Roseline prayed with gratitude in her heart.

Chapter Ten

Eleven years later...

Roseline lay in the tall grass on her blanket beneath a huge oak tree, listening to the birds and watching the puffy white clouds travel across the sky on a cool Saturday afternoon. She loved lying there, listening to the bees, smelling flowers, and helping herself to some orange juice. She lived in safety and peace, surrounded by people who loved her. And she particularly loved the outdoors in the spring when everything became alive again. She had lived here for ten years now and roamed the grounds like a young doe. They had sheep and cows and a proper barnyard on the far left of the property at the farmhouse. The hired hands who helped work the farm always smiled and waved at her whenever they saw her; she was a happy woman, free-spirited, and looked forward to each new day with a positive attitude knowing that the Lord daily loads His children with benefits.

"Hello, my lady. Have you been spoken for?" Her husband teased as he walked up, hugged her from behind, and kissed the back of her neck.

"Yes, my lord, Dr. Jim Kingston did that ten years ago; this one is off the market," she replied, turning in his arms to face him, batting her eyelids with a sassy smile on her face; she put her arms around her husband's neck.

Dr. Jim Kingston adored his wife, Roseline; he is like a child around her, even after ten years of being married to her with two children. She remained the center of his world and the object of his affection, and she felt exactly the same way about him. Most times, he sat gazing at her and thanking God for that fateful day he met her at the singles fellowship picnic eleven years ago; theirs was a remarkable and romantic story. They had gotten married after courting for a year. He'd bought the ranch in Delano, California, just before they got married; it was his wedding gift to her, and she absolutely loved it out there in the country, away from the city noise. They shuttled back and forth to Los Angeles only when necessary. He had a flourishing medical practice in Delano and served with his wife as their Church's Youth ministry leader in Delano. Once upon a time, she never could have believed this life filled with love was remotely possible, and here she was with this amazing, God-led man and two beautiful, thoughtful sons who are blessed with the most doting grandparents in the world – Evang. Anthony and Olivia Kingston, great-grandmother – Martha, and the sweetest aunt, Julia, with her daughter, Mary, whom her sons adore. Julia had gotten married to a lawyer, a good Christian man, Sam Harrington, in Los Angeles four years after Roseline got married. All this was like a dream come true, a dream she had never even had, but God gave it to her anyway, and she couldn't stop thanking God for all the ways He'd loved, saved, and blessed her. She was especially thankful for the amazing man He had used to give her everything she needed and nudged her to dream more, cheering her as she attained higher.

"We need to leave in an hour, sweety; it's quite a drive to LA, plus the traffic in the city; you don't want to keep the people waiting. Let's go get ready," Jim said, his hand around her waist as he led her toward the house.

They got to LA before 6:00 pm, dropped off their boys with Martha, who also was babysitting Julia's daughter so that Julia could attend the event, and by 6.45pm, they were seated in the hall.

The State Child Protective Services Director leaned toward the microphone, adjusting it slightly, and announced, "It is my privilege to introduce to you Dr. Roseline Kingston."

A hush fell over the hall, and the crowd of distinguished guests turned their attention to her. Roseline stood with practiced grace, and her husband walked her to the podium and returned to his seat. She placed her notes on the stand and felt the familiar rush of God's peace. Polite applause echoed through the room. The sea of faces was as familiar to her as she was to them; she was the voice of reason and faith in the dark world of child abuse, a wife and mother whose beliefs were clear as day and strictly one-sided against the will of the powerful – the side of the abused child. But they kept inviting and listening to her anyway because they knew she had something to say that was undeniably true. And most importantly, they knew her story – her horrific past, the abuse, the rejection, the sex slavery, the homelessness; she had personally lived the experience, and they were all aware of the pain she'd suffered and triumphed through it. She had earned tremendous sovereignty on this issue over the years with her authentic faith-filled voice, delivering something deeply moving and relatable to many who cannot speak for themselves.

They also knew she was no longer ashamed of her past; it was simply that – past. She walked now with dignity, having gone through school with the encouragement and support of her husband, Jim, who burnt the midnight oil with her, helping her study to get her General Educational Development (GED) first, agreeing to delayed childbirth for the first four years of their marriage to keep her focused on her education. She got into UCLA, graduated top of her class, and took it further to bag a master of Social Welfare and a Ph.D in Social Welfare to advocate and contribute to guiding policymakers and shaping practice and programs in such areas as children and families. Roseline also owned and managed six recovery shelters – RJ Kingston

Recovery Home, for abused girls across three cities in California, with the head office in Delano, where she spends most of her days. And through it all, Jim was her biggest cheerleader, and Martha never ceased to pray for her.

"Good evening, ladies and gentlemen," Roseline leaned into the microphone, flipping open her notes. Her eyes moved toward the left side of the front row, and she made eye contact with her husband; he smiled at her and nodded in solidarity.

"A little over a year ago, I met with and convinced the state child protective policymakers that it was time for a change; some of you at that meeting are here tonight," she paused, scanned the room, and some were nodding in acknowledgement.

"You agreed and offered the children a more robust program that has helped reduce the rate of child sex slavery and abuse," Her voice rang with a sincerity that flowed from deep within her soul. I am here today to remind you that this is only the first step; we need to do more to ensure that every child is fully protected and has access to a loving home and family, for that is the foundation of success for every child. If this foundation is stolen from a child and destroyed, you take hope and a future away from that child unless God intervenes in the story of such a child as He did mine, but not everyone gets that opportunity, and even when the opportunity presents itself, not everyone is convinced enough to accept it, Johnny never did, and he wasted his life abusing others like me and wound up dead on the streets like he was nothing. Johnny would still be here if only his childhood were protected; if only... his foundation was not destroyed," her voice cracked with emotion.

"Lord, give me the words to reach the hearts of these people – The heart of the king is in your hand, as the rivers of water: You turn it wheresoever You will," she prayed silently in her heart.

"My grace is sufficient for you," the words filtered into her heart, reassuring her, and Julia's eyes connected with hers, and she cheered her on with a thumps-up.

Roseline paused for a brief minute and scanned the room, registering the faces of those who had openly challenged the program over a year ago and noticed the change in their expressions tonight. The naysayers had viewed the program she'd presented to policymakers as a thinly veiled Christian program; thus, a violation of the separation of Church and State and a threat to free thinking and independent mindedness, but they appeared to be having a change of heart after listening to her emotionally charged delivery tonight and began to question their own motive for having challenged the program in the first place.

"The statistics of needlessly wasted young lives are daunting," she said as she read out the numbers from her notes. "When you leave this hall tonight, think about these numbers; the power to help these disadvantaged young ones are in our hands. Let's do the right thing. Thank you," she finished and stepped down from the podium.

Loud applause of respect rang through the room as everyone got on their feet for her. Jim stepped forward and led Roseline back to her seat before the room quieted down for the next speaker.

After the event, the press surrounded her with a barrage of questions. She calmly answered each of their questions, and Jim patiently stood by her side throughout the interview. Standing there watching her speak to the press, he was full of admiration and love for her, a smile playing around the corners of his mouth as he thought she was born for this, touching, and changing lives in ways only her personal experience can. After the interview, they headed to Martha's, where they had agreed to spend the rest of the evening with Julia and her family.

Martha opened the front door as they rang the bell, and they both hugged Martha, kissing her on both cheeks. They walked into the living room, laughing at the amount of noise in the house from the three children chasing one another and screaming. Julie and Sam were already seated in the living room, helping themselves to some orange juice. The four of them exchanged pleasantries and began to talk about the success of the evening's event. Then the men started to discuss basketball, and Julia excused herself to check on Martha in the kitchen.

Roseline stepped away and walked over to the window facing the street; the street where Martha had convinced her the early hours of that fateful morning long ago to take a step of faith to embrace life. The old lady unafraid and not caring that she could be a criminal, had opened her home to her at that ungodly hour of the morning, fed her, clothed her, helped her, accepted her, and loved her. Much later, when she had asked Martha why she was so unafraid to let a total stranger, who was a drug addict, into her home, especially being an old lady living alone in the house; Martha had shrugged and said, "Where there is perfect love, there is no fear because 'perfect love casts out fear' and the LOVE OF GOD is perfect."

Martha had also gone on to tell her with a confident smile, "The most powerful version of you is the 'you' that is fully convinced of God's love." How true those words are and how they have helped shape her own life today. Lost in thought, Roseline did not hear Julia walk up behind her until she touched her shoulder.

"You okay?" Julia asked, looking concerned.

"Yes, I am..." she smiled, "I was just thinking about the first time I got here and how you all accepted and loved me even with my mess. You and Martha's love for me brought me this beautiful life I have today; I got the best sister – you, the best grandmother – Martha, good education, a husband that adores me, and two wonderful sons. I got full restoration and some," she said with gratitude, "And I just want to do the same for other young people out there," she added, a long shaky breath left her lips.

"We were only vessels in the hand of God. But God alone rewrote your story, Roseline; He was the One who filled our hearts with love for you. God did it all, and He is already doing it for many young people in the RJ Kingston Recovery Home and others out there, using you with the love He has poured into your heart for them," Julia said with a shining sincerity.

Roseline felt her heart swell with love. She would share her story and life with everyone who needed it so they may come to know Christ and live life abundantly as Christ promised. Her life alone was proof that Christ was whom He said He was – the Savior, the Rescuer, God in the flesh. Because, indeed, it could only have been God who could have saved someone like her.

"Thank you, Jul, for being the sister I never had

nor even prayed for," she said, smiling broadly, "I love you, sis."

"That makes both of us; I love you too, sis," Julia replied, hugging her, and they walked back to join their men.

Jim put his hands around his wife, pulling her close; she leaned into him and placed her head on his shoulder, smiling as he kissed her head and heard her children's happy banter and laughter. Roseline sat nestled in the warmth of her husband's arms, feeling fulfilled and grateful; never for a second had Roseline dreamed that after the horrific events of her life, she would somehow wound up with a man like Jim – a humble, God-fearing, brilliant doctor and missionary. As if that wasn't heady enough, here she was surrounded by people who truly loved her. Indeed, God can immeasurably give His children access to more than they could ever imagine or ask.

The evening was sheer beauty, and it was time to leave. Since it was the weekend, Roseline and Jim agreed to the boys' and Martha's last-minute pleas for them to sleep over with her, and they would pick them up from Church the following day since Jim was going to minister at the headquarter Church in LA on Sunday on the invitation of the senior pastor. Change of clothes wasn't a problem; the children always had some clothes kept at Martha's.

Roseline sat beside her husband as they drove out of Martha's driveway and headed home. They drove in silence, not because they didn't have anything to say but because Jim understood her; he understood this was something she needed to savor – the feeling she had after spending time with her family. He held Roseline's hand, gently rubbing the back of her hand with his thumb and couldn't get the smile off his face.

"It's awesome... always so amazing," she said softly, smiling dreamily.

"Yes, it is," Jim replied, still smiling. He didn't have to ask what she meant; he understood.

This was what she'd missed all those years alone in the world; she'd missed more than she could ever comprehend. If only her mom knew better... if only..., she thought as a tinge of sadness attempted to creep in, but she shook it off; she wouldn't dwell on that, not now, not ever. God had richly blessed her; she had it all now in one single decision to say "yes" to God, and she knew He had more extraordinary things in store for her future. Being with her whole family together always gave her this feeling she never knew existed. The emotion was more than she could put into words. And Jim completely understood that. As the car slowed, and Jim turned into a long driveway that cut through a line-up of tall trees and headed towards a beautiful country house with a scooter and bicycle lying carelessly on the front porch, Roseline realized exactly what she was feeling and the words for it – "belonging". The feeling was that, for the first time in her life, she felt a sense of belonging, of being connected to people who truly loved and cared about her, not because of what she could do for them but because of who she was – simply Roseline! The feeling of love and acceptance finally – completely unpretentious.

Jim parked the car, got out and walked around to the other side to open the car door for his wife, smiling and taking her hand. Holding his hand, Roseline stepped out, smiling, pausing to look at their home, and the feeling became more evident with every step she took and every heartbeat because it was something she'd longed for since her happy childhood was stolen from her – the feeling of belonging, of family. And the feeling of being unconditionally loved and known by her name by the God of heaven and earth.

Epilogue

Philip squatted down by the young girl on the railway line, praying for her to make it while awaiting the paramedics. They arrived just in time as she passed out, bleeding from a cut on her head. They worked to stop the bleeding, binding up the head and raced her off to the hospital, generously allowing Philip to ride with her in the ambulance; she looked like she could use a friend.

At the hospital, she got checked in; thankfully, she was conscious enough to give her full name, Yasmine Davis. The cut on her head was deep and got stitched, and they took some blood samples to run some tests. After the tests and treatments, Yasmine got settled in a room. When the nurse asked if there was anyone that they could contact for her, she said she had no one, and Philip felt an even greater need to stay with her. She was thin, exhausted, wounded, and achy but able to listen, so he sat there talking to her, willing her to tell him how she'd come to be passed out on the railway while they waited for the doctor to return with some report on her situation.

A door opened behind Philip, and the doctor walked in with a folder under his arm; he stepped outside to give them privacy. A sense of fear overcame Yasmine on seeing the doctor; she glanced at the door behind him, leading to the hallway and outside. If only she could find the strength to get up, run out the door, tear down the hallway, and never stop; maybe she could end it all. It was pointless treating her for anything; she didn't want to be treated; she wanted to die so she could stay beyond the reach of David because he would always find her – he was too powerful and connected, and she couldn't stop him from hurting her. At that thought, panic shot a burst of adrenalin through her system, and she leaned forward, trying to get up, but the pain in her head pushed her right back on the bed as she moaned, holding her head. She was hyperventilating, letting panic have its way with her; she was wide-eyed, struggling, desperate for a way to escape the abuse, shame, and hurt.

"Code grey!" The doctor yelled, holding her down on the bed.

At that a nurse rushed in and gave her a shot. The shot calmed her in a few minutes, and she fell asleep. Philip stood outside the room, praying silently for her.

A few hours later, she awoke to Philip sitting beside her, praying. It took a while to remember where she was as he reassured her that she was safe, and strangely, a certain peace enveloped her as she nodded and smiled weakly at him. Later that evening, she shared her story with him.

Yasmine was a 19-year-old girl who wanted to end her life. She'd been orphaned since she was five years and had moved from one abusive foster home to the next. Tired of being abused, she had run away with a young man, David, who had promised her everything but given her only double the sorrow she experienced in the foster homes she'd run from. David, who was 15 years older than

Yasmine, would beat her to a stupor at the slightest and no provocation; he'd once stomped a pregnancy out of her, and she almost lost her life, and then he forced her to lie to the doctor that she fell down a flight of stairs, promising to kill her if she said otherwise. The last beating was the final straw for her; he'd smashed a bottle on her head, which is how she sustained the deep cut on her head. After he managed to stop the bleeding, he'd dropped her off at the ER to get stitched and waited in the parking lot to pick her up after she was done. She never saw a doctor; she saw an escape. A delivery truck was parked at the back, off-loading supplies through the back entrance and the driver had left the door open as he wheeled in some supplies; she snuck out the back door, running as fast as she could. Fleeing her abusive boyfriend, she'd ended up on the railway tracks with a pack of Hydrocodone she stole from the truck and swallowed some, hoping to have herself run over and killed by a train while she was numb to all pain and asleep. Yasmine was convinced at 19 that life held no meaning and nothing more for her.

Philip patiently listened to her. When she finished, there was a long silence between them. Clearing his throat, he stepped out of the room for a minute and returned with a young lady – he introduced Yasmine to Dr. Roseline Kingston, whom he had called on his way to the hospital in the ambulance to meet with Yasmine. Seeing Roseline in flesh and hearing her story, Yasmine let the dam of tears break loose as fresh hope and peace began to take root in her heart, hearing her quote the bible verse from Jeremiah 29:11 – *"'For I know the plans I have for you,' declares the Lord, 'plans to prosper you and not to harm you, plans to give you a hope and a future.'"* Yasmine treasured the notion in her heart, grasping to that shred of hope, daring to believe every word of it.

And with the help of the Holy Spirit, Philip shared the saving grace and love of Christ with Yasmine, as he'd done many years ago with Roseline. And realizing how much Jesus loved her by the way He loved Roseline and fixed her broken life to become the best, Yasmine accepted Jesus as her Lord and Savior that night. She was discharged from the hospital a few days later and Roseline had her checked into the RJ Kingston Recovery home, where she began to learn more about the love of Christ and His power to renew and restore.

157

A WORD FROM THE AUTHOR

We must learn to make our failures become our education if we must win the battle raging in our homes, in our hearts, for this primary education is the foundation for everything a person wants to be in life, for when the foundation is not stable, the future will be unstable unless God intervenes.

Thus, I have come to realize that everything we go through in life is for a purpose. God allowed us to go through it so that one day, we may be an encouragement to someone like Yasmine who had lost hope, drugged, and passed out on the railway tracks, waiting for the trains to run her over, but instead of death by suicide, which would have earned her a one-way ticket straight to hell, Yasmine met Jesus who restored her and gave her a new life.

No matter what you are going through, or whatever life throws at you, IF ONLY you would answer His call today and just lay it all down at His feet; IF ONLY you would allow Jesus – the burden bearer, to carry the burdens for you, and not try to struggle through life on your own, at the end of it, just as He had promised, He will give you rest. So don't lose hope, see an education in every failure, and most importantly, see Christ in everything.

Having read this story, now will be a good time to give your life to Jesus Christ as your Lord and Savior if you have not done that; it is never too late to do so. All you need to do is confess your sins, ask Him to come into your life, and be the Lord and Savior of your life.

God bless you now and always.

Oluseyi J. Akinlade